OUTLINES

OF

MEN, WOMEN, AND THINGS.

BY

MARY CLEMMER AMES.

NEW YORK:
PUBLISHED BY HURD AND HOUGHTON.
Cambridge: The Riverside Press.
1873.

RIVERSIDE, CAMBRIDGE:
STEREOTYPED AND PRINTED BY
H. O. HOUGHTON AND COMPANY.

To

MRS. PORTUS BAXTER,

OF VERMONT,

IN PRECIOUS MEMORY OF ONE GONE BEFORE,

These Papers

ARE AFFECTIONATELY DEDICATED.

CONTENTS.

I.	Arlington in May	1
II.	Northern Vermont in August	9
III.	Newport in September	20
IV.	Indian Summer in Virginia	37
V.	Charles Sumner's Home	43
VI.	Grand Duke Alexis in New York	56
VII.	A Rainy Morning in the Country	66
VIII.	Margaret Fuller Ossoli	77
IX.	A French Journalist	95
X.	Fanny Fern	106
XI.	Horace Greeley and Edwin Forrest	116
XII.	Lola Montez	124
XIII.	Things gone by	131
XIV.	The Fallen Man	144
XV.	Physical Basis of Statesmanship	155
XVI.	Instinctive Philosophers and Statesmen	164
XVII.	Pin-money	173
XVIII.	Breadmaking	188
XIX.	Our Kitchens	200
XX.	Caste in Sex	208
XXI.	Woman Suffrage	225
XXII.	Una and her Paupers	239
XXIII.	Let us Live	247

OUTLINES

OF

MEN, WOMEN, AND THINGS.

I.

ARLINGTON IN MAY.

ARLINGTON is a lovely spot. Virginia, with all its vaunting, can hardly boast of a fairer domain. From its slopes you look down upon the valley of the Potomac. Beyond the lordly river Washington stretches away to its crowning Capitol. The great dome glitters through the crystal-blue air, and high above it the Goddess of Liberty holds tutelary guard over the newly consecrated land. This is the picture — flecked here and there with breezy fields, and open woods, and softly swelling hills — which we see from Arlington. As we turned into the old Alexandria road, I thought of something that I saw not very long ago: a letter, the last one written by Mary Custis from Arlington, to Robert E. Lee, before she became his wife. The letter of a happy girl to the man beloved and chosen to be the husband of her heart and the ruler of her life, her eventful fate has given to it a touching significance. It referred solely to their approaching marriage and future life, and was full of love, and hope, and religious faith. The young officer, stationed for the time at Old Point Comfort, seemed to be in possession of only narrow quarters. Yet the heiress of Arlington saw nothing formidable in this, and counted it no sacrifice to leave the wide halls of her home for the scanty conveniences of a military fortress. "When mother came, why, they could make a bed in the sitting-room for *her;* and as for a maid, if there was no room, Mary Custis could do without one!" Rare self-abnegation for a Virginia heiress. Then came pleasant gossips about the bridesmaids and groomsmen already at Arlington, and maidenly fears as to how she should acquit herself through the trying ceremony; followed and finished with that exquisite humility of love which always sees in the beloved one the finer good, the diviner beauty, both of body and of spirit, which, humble-hearted, it misses in itself, only to recognize and worship in that other self who is now the counterpart and crown of all true existence.

She was unworthy of such great happiness;

but, because *he* deserved it all, the blessing of God would descend upon their union. Indeed, she felt that they could claim that benediction of heaven promised to those who honored and obeyed their parents, and sought to do the will of their Heavenly Father.

On a certain day she would ride from Arlington on horseback and meet him at Alexandria. Over this very road came the happy lovers. Far and fair on every side stretched the sunny lands which were their proud inheritance. Arlington House opened wide its doors to these beloved children. Its patriarchal trees waved their summer welcomes. Slaves came thronging from their cottages to greet their "dear Miss Mary" and her handsome young husband.

What a summer day for these joyous hearts! Ineffable as its sunshine shone the promise of their future. It was well for Mary Custis that to her was given no "second sight" to divine the sorrow of a far-off morning. Well that those soft eyes, looking on, did not see these gay old gardens and violet slopes sown thick with human bones, and turfed with ten thousand human graves! When she wrote this letter, in the sweet fullness of her heart, it was well she could not know that when her hair was white, and her heart old with many sorrows, a soldier would find this letter amid the treasures left in the home from which she was banished — banished because the husband for whose sake she dreamed all gracious fortune would come was an armed traitor, fighting against the government which had covered him with honor. She was innocent and lovely; but the innocence and loveliness of one could not avert the inevitable punishment of generations of wrong. This letter, full of all girlish gentleness and love, draws us in sympathy toward her who wrote it; yet we look on the graves of the dead, beneath the protecting trees of Arlington, and say, Far be that day when to Mary Custis, or to her children, shall be given back the home of her fathers!

"It would be enough to make these dry bones stir and come forth, armed with new life," said a gentle voice at my side this morning, in the Soldiers' Cemetery at Arlington. We stood on those wooded swards, looking down through the widening vistas, and on every side, reaching far out till they seemed to meet the sky, were the graves of our soldiers. No human tongue, though touched with the inspiration of angels, no word of man could move with the eloquence of this silence. From the fields of Manassas and Bull Run, from the thickets of the Wilderness, from the waste places of Virginia, day by day, the nation gathered her darlings, and laid them down to sleep upon these peaceful slopes. Thousands are buried here. Hundreds of thousands more, from the Heights of Arlington to the bayous of the Gulf, sow all the land — the soldiers who fought and perished for liberty. Every grave is turfed, and has at its head a white board, telling of the "unknown," or giving the name, regiment, and time of death of the soldier who sleeps below. At the entrance of the avenues are tablets, bearing inscriptions such as these:

"On fame's eternal camping-ground,
Our silent tents are spread,
And glory guards with solemn round
The bivouac of the dead."

. . . .

"Whether on the tented field or in the battle's van,
The grandest place for man to die
Is where he dies for man!"

I never saw Arlington so silent and lonely before. It is no longer the headquarters of troops, but a silent temple amid the vast city of the slain. The hush of the grave has touched its threshold. The sanctity of the dead seems to pervade its silence. The lower apartments are all open to visitors, who walk about with softened voice and step. The rooms look old and worn, but are in no way defaced. Old paintings still look down from the walls of the drawing-room, and in the library mouldy books are securely locked away in antique cases. The stag's head and antlers still deck the grand old hall, and a sideboard remains to tell of ancient cheer. Yet everywhere amid these relics of family life, with their stories of a happy and illustrious past, hang the records of our lost, reminding us only of the lowly yet illustrious dead. Beautiful Arlington, looking down upon a landscape soft as Italy, may you never again be the home of the living! The birds come earliest to your branches, and on your tender slopes the sweet arbutus first wakes to life. In your mossy moulds the violet distils its earliest fragrance, and here, when Summer seems gone from the world, she leans back to your sheltered hills to say good-by. There can be no kindlier spot in which the soldiers of our love may rest after the march and the battle. There can be no fitter place in all the world, than the domain of the man who used such power to destroy her, for the mausoleum of the nation.

Before me lies my first spray of trailing arbutus from the woods of Arlington. In Southern airs it caught its pinky bloom, filled its cells with honey, and distilled its subtle fragrance;

yet it is twin to the arbutus that I used to find amid the lush leaves and wonderful mosses of the woods of New York. Don't make me sentimental, Arbutus, with your memories of earlier Springs, from whose freshness neither time nor care had brushed the first dew of youth! You are the very same, Arbutus; you haven't grown old a bit. And Spring comes back, fair and young as ever. Time does not touch her bloom, nor palsy her pulses. The same ecstasy thrills in her veins, and in her myriad of delicate nerves young life is all astir.

Her loving angels are abroad. They tint the sky, soften the air, sail in the serene clouds. They have touched the buds, wakened the blossoms, they renew the life of the living; drop their mantles to cover the graves of our dead. How is it, Arbutus? You have not changed, neither has the Spring. We gaze on you with the same eyes, caress you with the same fingers; yet we, *we* are not quite the same. Each succeeding Spring seems to touch a deeper Spring of life within us. Every time we welcome May again we feel that we have gone down deeper into the mystery of Being. Our years need not be many to make us feel that they have robbed us. They have heaped up treasure for us. They have given us place and power, love and happiness. Yet they have buried our dead and estranged our living. They now make us feel what we have missed. They have taken from us that which they can never restore — the freshness, the promise of the beautiful beginning! Thus my Arbutus saith? You sin as you write, says Arbutus. My tender tints, my spiritual perfume, renewed in primal freshness Spring after Spring, are the promise of the Everlasting Spring.

II.

NORTHERN VERMONT IN AUGUST.

I FEAR I have nothing to say that you will in the least care to hear. I am just as fond of you as ever, dear souls; only I must own I am disinclined even to tell you so. Do you know how blessed it is to be quiet? How much more blessed it is to feel that you *may* be quiet in peace, that no mortal living has any right to demand that you shall break your peace by one compulsory word or sound? The latter blessedness I know not. I am at rest because I am a runaway. I have run away from the world. I am at peace because I will not be defrauded of it utterly by the wear and tear, the fret and hurry, the work and pain of mortal years lived in the trampling thoroughfares of men. Here am I watching a humming-bird oiling its gauzy wings in a spruce tree beside my window (such a charming sight), with not a word to utter of the slightest importance whatever. Not a thousand miles distant there is a little room whose desk and books and pictures and lounge even are full of serious meditation on human life and all that concerns it. Life has no phase of joy or pain, of thought, action, or experience, which has not been faithfully and often sorrowfully studied in that little room.

"The low sad music of humanity," the refrain of toiling millions of men and women, at times seemed too heart-breaking to be borne; the problems of human destiny too difficult and conflicting to be solved by mortal mind; the very comprehension of human life more than one could bear, sometimes, in that little room. When I shut its door I shut human life — at least, the ceaseless consideration of it — behind me. If this could never be done, how could one live? From this aerie in the mountains how can I reach down, take up its tangled thread, draw it into where I am, and weave it into the harmonies of thought? I am not here to think, but to rest; here to grow strong by fresh contact with the life-giving earth, to feed the very pulsations of life from the deep breast of the mighty mother.

I essay to speak; but can think of nothing but the brooks that I have waded and followed — the shining brooks, lined with moss, fringed with ferns, arched with cedars, spruce, and pines, thronged with trout, beautiful as flowers. I can see nothing but mountain tops and sunsets, and many lakes, glittering between the hills. Resplendent are these all to see; but oh! how poor they show through the finest glitter of words. Then it is heavenly to "loaf"; but it is not much to tell about. If it is loafing to bask on a bank, in the full blaze of the sun, through an entire August afternoon, making intimate acquaintance with bugs and "things" — the cunning workers of the ground and the murmuring nations of the air — then am I a born loafer. I spend an afternoon in this fashion whenever I can possibly get the chance. All the Aunt Jemimas in creation might croak around me about my waste of time, all the same I'd cultivate my bugs. Let the sun burn and tan me; I "loaf" on in imperturbability of soul. Pretty field-bugs, that live in the grass, are such delightful society, compared with tedious people. If you have never found this out, do try. My closest companions during the last month have been grasshoppers. They will not leave or forsake me. There is one actually hopping on my paper at this moment. The amount of time I spend in mending their legs and helping them out of tight places should insure me their gratitude as the benefactor of their race. "Grasshopper, grasshopper, give me some molasses!" is the child's cry. Now, unasked, they give me many other things — analogies among the rest. I sat down in an open field, the other day, amid grasshoppers as many as there are men in a State. The air was full of them, the brook was full of them, the grass was full of them, and by my side on an immense flat stone they were holding a mass meeting. They sat in rows, closer than the men in the Philadelphia Republican Convention. It was a serene looking assembly in mass. But very soon it gave evidence that it was not without its excited individuals, its "disaffected members." In sooth, it was not without its "bolters." My! When everything seemed to be progressing peacefully, up would hop a bolter and jump straight into the brook. Mad little bolter, he slid along smoothly enough for a minute; then whirls, eddies, rocks were his. On he dashed to his fate, straight into the mouth of a big trout.

Lake Memphremagog is set like a mirror between the mountains of Canada and Vermont. It has none of the warm sylvan beauty of Lake George, or of the idyllic loveliness of Lake Willoughby; but it has a majestic, masculine splendor wholly its own. When the September sun drops low, and cold, steely shadows creep along the sides of the girdling evergreen mountains, its deep, inky waters and lovely but lonely shores take on the look of the lochs of Scotland — blue, and cold, and solemn, like them. Under the frowning Owl's Head you feel as if you were sailing on Loch Achray and looking up at Ben Venue. But it has blither phases — long, bright vistas, filled with majesty and splendor, touched here and there with tender beauty. How I wish that I could transcribe them for you, so that the dead type might glow if but ever so faintly, with a reflection of the inexpressible beauty of God's world. But I am more and more impressed with the impotency of words in reproducing Nature, either in form or color.

"Why do we ever attempt it?" I ask a friend. "A painter cannot see a sight like this without the passionate desire to reproduce it in form or tint; or a writer, without the attempt to portray it in words. Both know before they begin that the best that they can do will be but a mockery of the reality. What makes them attempt it?"

"The instinctive desire to share it with others," was the answer.

The most attractive abode on the lake is that of Sir Hugh Alan, M. P. This is a story-and-a-half white cottage, standing on a hill, in a grove of white silver poplars, with the British flag waving proudly from its summit. This cottage, low and small, is nevertheless supported in true English state. When Sir Hugh, with his guest, Lord Lismeth, and a retinue of gay ladies, attend the little wooden church in the sleepy hamlet of Georgetown, dreaming a few miles further on, the fact is chronicled in the Stanstead newspaper with all the solemn *empressement* with which a sneeze of England's queen is recorded in the "Court Journal." Sir Hugh can go to church in his yacht. This little bantam steamer is the only lively thing on the lake. Compared with the graceful yachts which float in Newport Harbor, it is what a quacking duck is to a sailing swan. It quacks and waddles; but it waddles well.

Midway up the lake, on the Canada side, Georgetown clings to the shore, a barren, wooden, treeless little hamlet. At the end of it Magog — wooden, barren, and treeless, also, on a larger scale — waits the coming of the "Lady of the Lake," the only event of its Summer and early Autumn day. In Winter its days have no events. Here Mount Orford, the highest mountain in Canada, holds guard. And, while the boat turns, gazing back along the line of girdling mountains, through the vistas of embowered islands, which dot with gleaming emerald the sapphire of the lake, we see the towering and cloven notch of mountains in which shines that star of lakes, Lake Willoughby. The soil on the Vermont shore of the lake seems to be much softer, warmer, and richer than on the Canada side ; it has none of the blue, stony look of its precipitous banks, and this must account for the massy luxuriance of the foliage which covers its mountain sides, and crowns their summits, and curtains with the brilliant green of veiling vines the gray old bowlders which crowd the shore. The sun drops behind Orford a globe of scarlet, and the old mountain grows very purple in the face, and the top of his crown is edged with fire. We like his looks, which are somewhat exciting ; but the boat swings round and shuts him from sight. Here is old "Sugar Loaf." Every land that has a mountain at all is sure to have a Sugar Loaf ; but not every one beside one lake holds another on the top of his head. That is what this Mountain Loaf does. High above the rich cedars which skirt its sides, on its very summit, a tranquil lake holds up its mirror to the skies. The country folk call it Concert Pond, prized by fishermen in proportion to its difficulty of access, and to the choice quality of its speckled trout. We pass Owl's Head, beloved of mountains, to find the pretty White Mountain House at its base deserted, shut up, save when visited by picnic parties. Inaccessible by road, and visited but by a single boat, its actual loneliness and isolation have proved to be too great for the average summer tourists. Twilight on the waters deepens into the early September night. The boat darts through the darkness, in and out among the islands; the fishermen's huts fade out of sight on the shores; the shores merge into one dim and misty mass; Jay Peak is lost in the darkness of the skies; the little boy on my lap grows cold and still, then with a quivering sigh asks, "Where the big boat is going to, and if we will *ever* get home." And when, at last, it touches Newport pier, and I look back upon the dark water, shut within the imprisoning mountains, I am surer than ever that even in the sunshine Memphremagog, if one of the most beautiful, is also one of the most solitary of lakes.

Borne by loving arms Alice Cary was brought to this lovely lake-land during the last August of her life. From this bay-window she looked through a vista of maples out upon a broad expanse of meadow-lawn, whose velvet turf is of the most vivid malachite green, softened on its further edge by a grove wherein the shades of spruce and pine, elm and maple, contrast and blend. Beyond these woods Lake Memphremagog sets its glittering shield between the hills. On its farther side green mountains arise till they hold the white clouds on their heads. Below, Jay Peak stands over four thousand feet above the sea, while above, Owl's Head soars over three thousand, covered with forest to its summit. It is a picture fit for Paradise. Yet it is but one glimpse amid many, of the inexpressible beauty of this lake and mountain country of the North. She, sitting here, looked out upon this consummate scene; looked with her tender, steadfast eyes across these emerald meadows, to the lake shining upon her through the opening hills, to the mountains, smiling down on her from the distant heaven, their keen amethyst notching the deep, deep blue of a cloudless sky. The splendor of this northern world fell upon her like a new divine revelation. The tonic in its atmosphere touched her feeble pulses; the peace brooding in its stillness penetrated her aching brain with the promise of a new life. Without, the world was full of tranquillity; within, it was full of affection and the words of loving kindness. Then she wondered (and her wonder was sad with a hopeless regret) why Summer after Summer, she had lingered in her city home, till the crash and roar of the streets, coming through her open windows, had filled body and brain with torture.

"How blind I was," she exclaimed. "I said that I could not take the time from my work; and now life has neither time nor work left for me. How much more, how much better I could have worked had I rested. If I am spared, how differently I will do. I will come here every Summer and *live.*"

Alas! before another Summer, the winter snow wrapped her forever from the earthly sight of this unutterable beauty.

Hers, from the beginning, was the fatal mistake of so many brain-workers — that all time given to refreshment and rest is so much taken from the results of labor; forgetting, or not realizing, that the finer the instrument, the more fatal the effects of undue strain, the more imperative the necessity of avoiding over-wear and the perpetual jar of discordant conditions; forgetting, also, that the rarest flowering of the brain has its root in silence, and beauty, and rest.

Here in this window, whither, wasted and suffering, she had been borne, she wrote her "Invalid's Plea": —

"O Summer! my beautiful, beautiful Summer,
I look in thy face and I long so to live;

But, ah! hast thou room for an idle new-comer,
  With all things to take and with nothing to give?

"With all things to take of thy dear loving-kindness,
  The wine of thy sunshine, the dew of thy air;
And with nothing to give but the deafness and blindness
  Begot in the depths of an utter despair?

"The little green grasshopper, weak as we deem her,
  Chirps day in and out for the sweet right to live;
And canst thou, O Summer! make room for a dreamer,
  With all things to take and with nothing to give?

"Room only to wrap her hot cheek in thy shadows,
  And all on thy daisy-fringed pillow to lie,
And dream of the gates of the glorious meadows,
  Where never a rose of the roses shall die?"

III.

NEWPORT IN SEPTEMBER.

I HAVE reached "the land where it is always afternoon." Even when the morning sunshine splinters on the keen-blue waves of the bay, and its expanse is full of motion and sound, there is a quality in the atmosphere, a softness in its light which falls upon you and pervades you like the tranquillity of evening. It is born of tempered elements. I cannot tell you what it is; but it is full of rest. It is not wonderful that this is named the Isle of Peace, or that tired people like to come here. As I take my morning air-bath on this little family pier, I find a fascination in these waters that will not let me go. It soothes brain and nerves. It silences the rush and roar of the great, hurrying world. It says: "All things have rest from weariness. All things have rest; why should *you toil* alone?" I conclude that I won't. The truth is, I can't. The result is, the mail closes, the boat departs, and the light of heaven, the voices of earth, the mesmerism of the waves, the pictures of human life, all thronging together void and voiceless in the mind, have refused to take on palpable shapes, and have disdained the feeble offer of a stubby little pen to reveal them. I'd send you the crown of the morning, if I could. An hour ago it looked like a storm, and the wind blew perversely. It was only a make-believe of the Nereids. They are busy now lifting up the steely fog that covered the bay like a shield; and, as its edges break and curl and fly away to the sun, they glitter like shreds of silver. Underneath spreads the bay, a translucent sapphire. In the bay float the jelly-fish — tremulous, gleaming jewels. On the waves the fishing-punts are putting out for their heavy shoals. The bay-skiffs are all on the wing, darting from the little household piers and dancing away for a swing in the wake of some stately steamboat. Row-boats, painted bright blue and red and yellow, are darting about in every direction, full of boys and girls, whose happy voices come back to us across the waters.

Down the harbor a little way the idle yachts lie dreaming with the sleeping gales, before they begin their mid-day race. Beyond, past old Fort Louis, a great school-ship from New York has cast anchor. What a sight it is — the hundreds of boys clinging like bees to its mighty yards. High up in the blue air, they look no bigger than bees; and I watch them dropping, dropping like spiders down their ropy stairs.

Now four long black boats are dropped down the ship's sides to the water. Now they are filled with boys, and now they scull across the bay for a race; while a thousand boys on the ship fill the air with their shouts and hurrahs. Away out to the ocean these bright waters are quick with human life. But human life upon the waves is not the noisy and tiresome thing that it is upon the streets. The very motion — clear, swift, and silent — is full of repose. It reminds me of delicious Venice, that I never saw. What would be these primeval elements alone, without the human presence, that loves and suffers, rejoices and sins? Midway in the bay lies the green island of Canonicut. I see a church-spire, and clustering farm-houses, and sunshiny meadows, and cattle grazing down to the very shore. Below, the stone ramparts of Fort Adams, with their mounted guns, rise from the water; and nearer Fort Louis lifts its gray old head above the soft, purple "Dumpling" hills. So perfect a picture of it as Higginson has given us in "Malbone" can never be made again. He says: "As you stand upon the crumbling parapet of old Fort Louis, you feel yourself poised in middle air; the sea-birds soar and swoop around you; the white vessels come and go; the water is around you on all sides but one, and spreads in pale-blue beauty up the lovely bay, or in deeper tints southward toward the horizon-lines. I know of no ruin in America which Nature has so resumed; it seems a part of the original rock; you cannot imagine it away."

It is a single low tower, shaped like the tomb of Cæcilia Metella. But its stately position makes it rank with the vast sisterhood of wave-washed strongholds. It might be King Arthur's Cornish Tyntagel; it might be "the teocallis tower of Tuloom." The pretty *Mermaid* carried us over to it the other day — a perfect day. She bore us into a moss-covered cove, and we climbed the slippery rocks, led by a maid with flowing hair and a scarlet petticoat. How gay and picturesque she was against the gray old summit, as she looked back and called us on! We sat down at last upon the broken parapet, high above the water — a little company, each of whom sent "long, long thoughts" of his and her own silently out to the questioning waters. We were enveloped in the marvelous atmosphere (fine, soft, sun-suffused, yet exhilarating) which has made the climate of Newport famous for centuries. Across the bay, Newport soared from shore to hill, lovely as that enchanted City of the Sea portrayed in "Counterparts." At either end of the islands far-away lawns run from villa and *châlet* down to the bay, with white yachts tossing by the pretty piers at their feet. Just below us a pleasure-boat, filled with a gay party, was running in and out among the rocky islands and coves of the "Dumplings." Before us a French corvette was lying in the stream, its tri-color hanging disconsolate in the still air, and its Gallic hands busy at work making haste to leave an unfriendly port. On the other side of us, the sheep were grazing on the rugged slopes of Canonicut. Within the fort Nature's wild blooms covered with grace the *débris* at our feet. Roving bees hummed to us with assiduous attempts at more intimate acquaintance. Crickets trilled their slender horns in the waving grasses, while all around us the golden-rod on the crumbling bastions waved its yellow sceptre and proclaimed to us that the conquering Autumn had come, and taken captive the Isle of Peace, no less than the lanes and woods at home.

Ah, my dears, it is so hard to work here — so very hard. I try ; but every day some lovely gust of human kindness swoops me up and sweeps me away. Again the mail closes, the boat goes, and — and you know the rest.

Let me think, and see if I can tell you a few of the lovely things that have happened since I stopped up yonder; but, if I were to take up again every sunny thread that I dropped, I couldn't weave them into a picture at all.

There was the out-door lunch-party at Mrs. Julia Ward Howe's country home, six miles away. It was all that a lunch-party could be on the fairest of August days, under the trees, with a ruined mill at the foot of the hill; and handsome men and beautiful women and flower-like girls basking on the grass; and the most genial of "high-up" philosophical doctors from Boston to hold them in a mild degree of awe, and to preserve them from degenerating into too absolute mutual admiration; and with a hostess to whom "Kant" is "light reading" and the Sanskrit a pastime, dispensing chowder with lavish ladle. I bear witness that she did it gracefully, generously, with those beautiful hands, and without a hint of ink or of "Moral Trigonometry." Mrs. Howe is attractive anywhere. Even on the platform she appears with a shy, half-deprecating, half-bewildered air, as if she herself could not quite make out why she was there; but nowhere else does she appear to such absolute advantage as she does when dispensing hospitality to her friends, in her own demesne, in the midst of her young daughters, each one of whom is a perfect wild-rose in her fresh, girlish grace.

I will here ask Mrs. Howe why, instead of doling out her essays to scanty audiences, she does not set them within book-covers and give them to the world? They belong to American literature, and ought to take their place in it. Nothing to compare with them in scholarship and philosophical thought has been produced by any American woman except Margaret Fuller. At present the highest feminine gifts in this land, as well as much of the masculine, through the exigent demands of daily life and the curse of the want of money, are devoured by that insatiable Moloch, the Press, who still cries for more, but makes no record of the untold treasure which he devours. How many grandly-endowed women sacrifice the rich vitality of their heart and brain to this monster, day by day; yet they must pass and leave no enduring trace in the world of art of all that they have thought, felt, suffered, and given to their race. With all her mental and spiritual wealth, no American woman to-day is giving anything that will long endure to the literature of her country. Thus, if there is one among us who *can* embody for the world the best results of leisure, of culture, of comprehensive thought, and of rarest womanhood, let us have it.

How I wish that I could transcribe for you the splendor of "the Cliffs." But in these September days there hovers a light over sea and shore which cannot be caught and imprisoned in words. Wordsworth would not have sung of "the light that *never was* on sea or land" had he gazed out over this opaline ocean, over these flickering shores, which in the same moment concentrate and radiate the loveliest of unimagined, indescribable hues. The beach, two weeks ago crowded with equipages and gay people, the surf, alive with hundreds of shouting and laughing bathers, are empty and forsaken. The gale swept away the long line of bathing-houses; the pie and candy man has gone to assist elsewhere in the destruction of the human teeth and stomach; but "the Cliffs!" — never in the July heats was their beauty so absolute as in the perfect sunshine under the perfect heaven of this September morning! Yonder, amid the abundant grass, the peaceful cattle graze; yonder a maple beckons us toward it with a scarlet hand: yonder wide beeches and elms spread out green tents under which we may rest. Amid these, its face toward the sea, looks forth a home so harmonious in outline, so poetical in aspect, that it is hard to realize that the trail of death and sorrow could ever pass through it, or that those who inhabit it could ever be tired or sorry, sick or lonesome, as at some time every mortal who carries the burden of this human life must be. Past hundreds of such homes, on and on through the green grass, for miles winds the narrow path of "the Cliffs." The absolute peace of the green earth and its homes on one side; ragged rocks, evermore the ocean on the other. What stories you would tell, little path, if you only could! What vows, what love you have listened to, perhaps by those who uttered them so long ago broken or outlived! What beauty you have seen, what purity, what sin! What human want, and loneliness, and sorrow, and joy have told their stories to you! At the boat-house, over two miles from its beginning, the path of "the Cliffs" ends. Here, above the sheltered cove where the little boats are chained to the rocks, looking toward Brenton's Reef, where the lightship tosses through the nights and days, you may sit down, and with your gaze try to follow the ocean out to where it meets the horizon. To do this is to relinquish yourself to its spell, to be magnetized by its might. It draws you outward into its infinity. You catch a glimpse of your own eternity. "Long, long thoughts" are these which leave your soul to travel out across its immense reaches of ever-shifting space. No narrow street, no imprisoning walls limit or restrict your mind as it goes on to the eternities. You are the same being that you were yesterday in the stifling and crowded city — the one who then felt so inadequate to live; the one to whom life, with its penalties, its losses, its pain, seemed so much more than you could bear. How feeble seemed your hold on human love, on thought, on spiritual faith! You are the very one — and now! How certain you are of everything sweetest, truest, and best. Already you have passed through "the sea change into something rich and strange." You sat down beside it, weary in body, weary in heart; and unaware you have already drawn into your veins something of its inexhaustible life. This is one talisman of the ocean, its boundless energy. Who can approach its waves and not feel it and receive it! It electrifies you forever with its buoyancy of life. Ages of storms cannot make it old. After every tempest, it comes back and touches your pulses and washes your feet with the smile of irrepressible youth. Yet its very waves, as they break before you, have something eternal in their call. As you follow them, how sure you feel that there is that in you which can never end. How sure that the love and devotion of your throbbing heart will survive when that heart is still. How sure that the beings best beloved — marred now by the infirmities of the body and of the mind — will yet be given to you some day redeemed and glorified and pure.

To those who seek it, there is a charm in Newport beyond its fashion. The Ocean House is closed. The gay pagoda, where the band played a week ago, is silent. The great halls and piazzas, then thronged with gay promenaders, are shut and deserted. No six-in-hand now dashes along Bellevue. The Turk, with his toys from Constantinople, has gone; the fashion shops have hurried back to Broadway; but Newport is lovelier far than when all the denizens of Babylon were here. The cottagers remain; and the cottages, their flowers, their velvet lawns, their hammocks swinging toward the sea. Redwood Library — that perfect *bijou* of a library — is still here, and more enticing than ever. One may sit in an easy-chair and read almost any newspaper or review *ad libitum*. You may look at the "Dying Tecumseh;" or if you don't want to, at "Venus of Milo" and "Apollo Belvidere." The fashion has gone; but the ocean remains, and the perfect days. There is a softer iterance in its call than ever came to us in Summer. A light rests upon its waves and on its shores which no language can interpret or transfigure. Along the roadside crowds of asters look up at us through their purple eyes, while all around them every knoll and meadow flames with golden-rod. In the tree-tops the miracles of color have begun. Autumn, in her first ecstasy, has decked herself as for a carnival in yellow and scarlet. From its floods the Island has emerged as radiantly green as when June was born. All around it run the opal lines of the ocean; all over it bends the intense blue of the heavens, flecked with the ever-changing splendor of the sailing clouds. Within, enthroned are these superlative days, "Mediterranean days," whose golden airs flow over you and through you, full of the softness, without the languor of the South. Here by my open window, looking over Narragansett Bay to the ruined forts which Higginson has so inimitably portrayed, I am reading "Malbone." I should never have read it if I had not come to Newport. For, dipping into it in the "Atlantic" one day, I touched Malbone and recoiled. I have a constitutional hatred of a masculine Mormon. If I had my way, there is not a willful, intelligent man-Mormon in this land that should exist in it a moment longer than it would take to drive him out of it. But the Mormon whom I especially detest flourishes outside of Utah, makes mischief and havoc far from the walls of Salt Lake City. He is especially detestable because, besides being a Mormon, he is a hypocrite. A Mormon in practice, he yet pretends to be something else and better. Malbone is a constitutional Mormon. Nothing but laziness and the laws could keep him from having a harem fuller than the Sultan's. Missing this, he would console himself by prowling into other folds, and none could be too sacred for him to invade. No noble work or ambition absorbs his manhood. All the subtlety of his intellect, all the graces of his person, are valuable to him only as they enable him to manipulate the hearts of women; and the sole study and profession of his life is to make all women of any charm his slaves. If any woman on earth is unfortunate, it is she who loves with a woman's pure, sole love such a man — a man who loves (?) her only while he sees her, and forgets her altogether while kissing the next woman that he meets. This is Malbone, altogether contemptible from beginning to end. One is thankful that his victims are portrayed in such pale water-colors that one can suffer less for them than if they were living women, embodying in life-force their agony and wrong. "Malbone" and "Aunt Jane" are real — the only vitalized characters in the book. In reading it, one feels certain that the man who wrote it ought to and can write a vastly better one; that where it is thin and weak it is so through no paucity of material, but through the hesitation of the author to use the material that he had. It is written in delicious English. Its words are pure and limpid as this Newport air. Its Proem is perfect. And in a hundred exquisite touches it reveals and portrays the varied loveliness of this enchanting placo with a sympathy and charm which has never been surpassed. Opposite is the old "Hunter House," in which its scenes were placed; a noble old house, looking out through its trees with wide-open doors, as if it had no secrets to hide. All Summer it has been filled with boarders — mothers and their children. Its great hall runs straight through the middle, and its front-door and back-door stand wide open from morning till night. I look through it now, away out to the bay. Any of us and all of us race through it, down to the little pier behind the house. After reading Higginson's poetic description of this old colonial mansion, I ran across the street and studied it — its carved mahogany staircase; the pineapple above its back-door; the dumpy cherubs on its parlor wainscot, which, by the way, some barbarian has painted white; even the spiral stairs up which poor little Emilia is supposed to have crept to the handsome but good-for-nothing Turk in the attic. Now they are very honest-looking stairs, without the suggestion of secrecy; their doors, opening on every hall, matter of fact white doors, which look as if they never could have shut in either tragedy or shame. Colonel Higginson lives a few streets back from the bay, in a cottage *ornée*, amid flowering baskets, trees and vines, books and pictures, as a poet should. The master of a perfect style, if he does not break his power on too small matters, and waste it in petty punctilios, he ought to give us the best American novel since the days of Hawthorne.

It is Saturday, September 3, and the event not only of the season of 1870, but of years, has come to Newport. The Spouting Rock is sending up water in cataracts, and a great storm at sea has come up to the shores. All Newport is at the ocean. For miles the ocean-road is thronged with equipages. Gentlemen and ladies scale the cliffs on horseback, while thousands stand and sit upon the rocks, silent with awe. The sky is steely gray. The clouds hang low and cold, rushing athwart and repelling each other. The waves rise, roar, strike, and resist each other; the elements are all at discord. What is the matter with the ocean?

> "In name of great Oceanus,
> By the earth-shaking Neptune's mace,"

what *is* the matter? A thousand Niagaras let loose chase each other to our very feet. Great, green, glittering walls of wave, they rise far out, moving slowly, slowly on; reaching higher, higher, as they come; till, full before us, quivering, toppling, they rush upon the rocks; rise, lash, break, and lash again, with stupendous roar. Other waves, distinct and individual as animate beings, dart up from the ocean, and, with white manes far outspread, absolutely fly above the water. Fleet, terrible is their race, these chariots of the sea, with Triton their trumpeter, till in swift collision they strike, and lie shattered on the shore.

Pan is not dead. The Ocean of God is moved to its deepest cavern, crying aloud, as if it knew the message which it this instant bears of the folly and misery of man. This moment the electric chord within it is repeating to the world another of the awful tragedies of history, as Napoleon III. the Man of Destiny, imbecile and old, succumbs at last to fate; and men beloved, the sacrifice of kings, lie slain on a hundred battle-fields.

IV.

INDIAN SUMMER IN VIRGINIA.

TELL me, please, when Indian Summer comes. The trouble is, I never found any one yet quite certain when its perfect days dawn and fade away from the world. It must be that Indian Summer comes, and goes, and comes again, at her own gracious and golden will, through all the months of October and November. In early October, when its scarlet conflagration spreads from mountain to mountain, till they blaze from base to summit; when the first veil of mist floats over their tops, and the first golden nebulæ sails down the valleys; when the physical and spiritual sense within us is first touched by that coolness and stillness, that softness and sadness, which, penetrating the fervor of the later Summer, *is* Autumn—then our newspapers and our neighbors tell us that it is the beginning of the Indian Summer.

But a whole month later, when the color carnival is nearly ended, when the intense scarlets and ambers have burned into ashen hues;

when the evergreen of pine and cedar, the garnet of the oak, alone throw rich shadows across lingering lichens and the purpling grays of autumnal mosses; when crows caw in dismantled woods, and squirrels scamper through their rustling lairs, and nuts drop into their russet beds, and the crickets pipe their shrilly horn in the yellow grass, and the wide atmosphere seems palpitant with limpid gold, and the finest pulses within us tremble, touched by the finest phases of sight, and sound, and of subtle fragrance—then from the hills, or the heavens, we know not which, falls that dream-like spell which seems to hold all things in peaceful trance, and we stand as in a vision amid the transfigured world. We are awed by its miracle, and no one need tell us that it is Indian Summer. This season reaches perfection amid the Virginian hills. It comes early and lingers late. Its delicious coolness pervades you like a presence before you behold a visible token of its advent. I saw its first little scarlet flag, waving from the top of a sumach tree, weeks and weeks ago. It was not September then. Yet it was on that grassy ridge, over which the little red flag fluttered, that I caught my first autumnal glimpse for you. Through the trees which fringed it I saw marvelous glimpses of the Shenandoah, with its sea-green gleam, flashing at intervals far up the valley; and on either side the first mountains of the Blue Ridge lifted their softly-scolloped edges toward the deeper sky. Yet it is not for these that I would have you see what I saw. It is very sentimental, you know, wandering about searching for views; and you and I wish to be practical and wise! Let no imagination touch these broken ramparts, these deserted forts, these high-piled earthworks, looking as if they had been thrown up but yesterday; these rifle-pits, these battered canteens, these flattened bullets lying in the grass, these scattered graves. Three years ago this fragrant wood-way was alert with manly life. Great guns pointed toward that lonely river; bayonets glistened above those low-boughed oaks. Five years ago this hour I saw the sun set below these mountains, swathing these steeps in peaceful light, crowning with sacrificial glory ten thousand men in line of battle before the foe. The fight was deadly. Man mocked the peace of God with the impotence of war. The shock of cannon shook these hills. Shells ploughed the serene ether with fiendish yell. Musketry rattled. Everywhere around us were the dying and the dead. Far as the sight could reach, along the white road, in ghastly line, moved "the anguish-laden ambulance." Through the twilight, through the starlight, pierced the cry of the wounded. My God! Who that *ever* heard it can forget!

And *now?* The sumach waves its scarlet flag above that battle-ground. That battle-ground where so many knightly hearts beat and bled, where so many fair young lives went down in sacrifice, was now gay with golden-rod. The wild-rose blossomed in the covert of the fort; on the very edge of the rifle-pit the evening primrose held up its cup of gold. And *now?* Through the purple haze we look away to Maryland Heights and Loudon Mountain. We lift our eyes to old South Mountain, and behold still the furrows through its woods which the batteries cut that day. Below us Antietam Creek maunders through the meadows. There is Burnside's Bridge, and, on the Sharpsburg side, the ancient church into which the wounded were carried from the battle-field. Here, in God's quiet, sleep the dead of Antietam. *The dead?* It is the living who are dead; who are false to the cause for which they perished. Ten thousand sleep together here. Look at the long, long trenches! They who are buried in them, in such close embrace, died in the thickest of the fight; and no power can gather their names from oblivion. "Aged nineteen," "twenty," "twenty-one," and "twenty-two"! Thus we walk on, and on, and find no record which tells that the soldier below lived twenty-five earthly years. Was it not the flower of the people, in truth, that perished for country and the humanity of man. The battle still goes on. The old, old battle of truth and falsehood, of might with right, of corruption with the incorruptible. On the anniversary of that battle, when the nation agonized for its life, demagogues, who have betrayed every sacred principle for which these soldiers died, dared to profane the silence of their rest by shouting words of party rant and of political intrigue above these graves. I looked on their bloated faces, and beside them came other faces — powder-grimed, death-pale, imploring-eyed — the faces of men that I saw die. It was grief unfeigned that cried: Was it for this, *only this*, you perished, O my land's beloved! O ye living, do you realize the cost of every prize which Freedom holds precious? Then let us dedicate ourselves anew to be worthy of our heritage. Only through a manhood and a womanhood consecrated, exalted, can we prove to after ages that our dead died not in vain.

It is through individual purity "that the nation shall, under God, have a new birth of freedom; and that governments of the people, for the people, shall not perish from the earth."

Since that September evening what superlative days have trailed their splendors along these mountain-sides! They linger still. As I see the great pines on the mountain-tops dip their needles in the gold of the ascending sun, I say, "Another matchless morning! It must be the last!" And when the sun drops down the valley, and its sentinel mountains change from amethyst to amber, and vale and river are flushed with unimagined hues, I say "Italy cannot more than mate this sunset! But there cannot be another!" Yet the perfect days have merged into weeks, and still the miracle goes on. It is as if Summer — not the impassioned queen whose ensanguined death we watched upon the mountain yonder; but another Summer, serener, softer than the first — smiled in the very face of Winter, brightening the world ere she leaves it forever.

V.

CHARLES SUMNER'S HOME.

The eastern sunshine pouring down upon the blooming city does not add its brightness to any spot in Washington so pleasant as that lying within the compass of Arlington Hotel, Lafayette Square, and the Executive grounds and mansion. In Winter, or Spring, or Autumn the scene here is always metropolitan and beautiful. Within this radius are the winter homes of Mr. Sumner, Vice-President Colfax, General Fremont, General Irwin, General Butler, General Bancroft, Secretary Belknap, Speaker Blaine, Secretary Fish, and many other public persons. The asphalte pavement scarcely sends back a sound, yet it is covered with glittering equipages and thronged with richly-dressed women and children, while the ample halls of the Arlington are perpetually sending forth a gayly dressed and distinguished throng.

But in April, without warning, Lafayette Square breaks into a sudden splendor which makes all mortal splendor poor. The trees which line and arch the street on either side take on a sudden glory which shames the bare and chill arcades of their northern brethren. Never was there a deeper depth of bloom than that which draws and holds the vision in these deep blossomed trees. I never gaze into them without thinking what they would have been to the eyes and souls of De Guerin and Thoreau. They slowly sway their green pendants against the gold of the evening sky, and the very movement soothes one like the music of content.

The sunshine, glimmering through the green roof of the park, enters the eastern windows of a house opposite, and, hovering over its pictures and works of art, seems to flood its rooms with somewhat of that light which never was on sea or shore. It needs all the potency of the eastern sun to bring out upon these canvases the full glory of color, and to suffuse the tints of the artist with the vivid splendors of actual Nature. On these walls hang original paintings by Tintoretto, Sir Peter Lely, Sir Joshua Reynolds, Sir Benjamin West, Gerard Douw, Gainsborough, with a captivating collection of proof engravings. In the large back parlor, half-dining, half-drawing-room, the fine light of the morning shines full upon one of the material beauties of the court of Charles the Second, and upon the portrait of Hannah More, at thirteen, by Sir Joshua Reynolds — two portraits of opposite types of womanhood, the latter preëminent in intellectual beauty, showing a face in coloring and expression never to be forgotten.

On the easels in the bay-window we see a group of Spanish officers in a Holland guard-house. They are smoking their pipes and holding up wine-cups in their exquisite hands, as if reveling in mirth and "dreamful ease," in utter oblivion of a Dutch guard-house. Opposite, the Holland lacemaker sits in her open porch. Without, there is a glimpse of summer sky; its tranquil light peers in and plays upon her placid face. It is the realization of repose. There is rest in the movement of the soft hands weaving the thread above the pillow, and in the very dog asleep at her side. Between these homely pictures of realistic life stands the marble daughter of a king.

> "She was so beautiful that, had she stood
> On windy Ida by the oaken wood
> Troy might have stood till now with happy days,
> . . . And Psyche is her name in stories old."

An exquisite life-size marble, copied from the antique original at Naples.

In a painting over the mantel a god is descending to break the chains of a slave. Here are a portrait of Benjamin Franklin, busts of Longfellow and of Everett, while engraved heads of many of the masters of the world line the wall from floor to ceiling. In another part of the room fruits and flowers suggest beauty and cheer. Everywhere there is color and warmth. High ideas and the forms of beauty are alike embodied in the tints and outlines of art. Yet all are toned into harmony under one artistic hand. Nothing seems too beautiful to be enjoyed, and the aspect and atmosphere of the room are not more poetical than homelike. But the adjoining apartment is preëminently the scholar's room. You pass its open threshold, to stand bewildered, on the first glance, at its profusion of bronzes, busts, statuettes in marble, antique souvenirs, various vases, photographs, engravings, and paintings. Yet the carpet under your feet is true to the suggestions of Nature, as all carpets should be — softly green as the May turf, covered with golden stars, like the dandelions dotting meadows. One side of the room is hung with engravings from Turner; and here is the ancient head of young Augustus, from which all the portraits of the first Napoleon were modeled. Here is the marble bust of

Mr. Sumner, taken in 1839, while he was editor of the "American Jurist;" here the winged Mercury, the Venus of Milo, Hercules, Demosthenes, Pericles in his veiling helmet, with kings, philosophers, and dreamers of many ages and climes. Above the bookcase hangs a painting which pervades the entire room with its delicious atmosphere, It is an Italian landscape, by Richard Wilson, the English Claude.

Apart from its exquisite coloring, it attracts and holds one through "the subtle secret of the air" — that depth of distance which draws the sight on, and on, and on; that marvel of perspective which seems to allure us into eternity in the pictures of Turner. But the choicest treasures lie out of sight, as choicest treasures always do. When these softly shutting drawers are opened, they show many a quaint illuminated book; a Bible bound in wood, written on parchment by some monkish hand, with the iron chain which held it to the ancient public reading-stall still hanging to it. Here are mediæval missals, wrought on vellum, with many a flowering saintly device, bound in velvet and clasped with gold, just as they were when some lady prayed over them at the altar in the dim past. Here is a diploma given from the University of Padua, generations since, which bears every mark of having been a family treasure. It is bound in crimson velvet, its Latin printed in gold, its pages illuminated with flowers as brilliant in tint as if they had just grown under an artist's hands. The portrait of the youth to whom it was given looks forth from under this gorgeous cover. Fresh and fair in immortal youth is this son of Padua, though all of him mortal went back to dust long ago.

There is nothing on earth more stupidly dull than an average autograph book. The vast crop grown in Washington certainly has not increased their value; but here are faded names, written on parchment scrolls, which stir a thousand nameless memories. The very sight of them seems to people the place with the men and women who made the epochs of this world's history. Here is a deed in Latin, signed by Elizabeth, Queen of England. This overtopping "E" and imperial flourish were traced by the vain and haughty hand of the tyrannical queen. I won't moralize over it; but it *has* suggestions. So also has this, the name of her brutal father, Henry VIII., traced by his own hand. Here is a veritable letter written by Catherine De Medicis to her son, Charles IX.; and here the picture of this woman, great in guile — a handsome woman, with a flattened head and a material face, and a stately form, cased within a closely fitting robe, likes the scales of a serpent. Here also is a letter from Mazarin to Fabri de Peirese, written from Avignon, 1634, and another from Richelieu to the Marquis of Breze, 1632. And these are but a few of the names in this priceless collection. It is like thrusting one's hand back into a far-off age, and drawing something out of its silence, to lift this little book from the drawer wherein it lies. It is called an "Album Amicorum," and was kept by a Neapolitan nobleman, Camillus Cordoyn, at Geneva, during the first half of the 17th century. This town being on the highroad to Italy, at that time, it was a favorite stopping-place. This album contains several hundred autographs of different nations, each with a motto or sentiment attached. Among these are those of German princes, French noblemen, English Cavaliers, and Roundheads. This is the inscription by the famous Lord Strafford, when a young man, on his continental tour: "*Qui vivit notus omnibus ignotus moritur sibi*, 1612." John Milton, on his way back from Italy, shortly before his return to England, wrote in this book the last line of his own "Comus," which was already published before he began his travels.

Here it is in Washington to-day, 1871, its freshness scarcely dimmed, as sensitive and delicate in characters as the day on which they were traced: —

> "If virtue feeble were
> Heaven itself would stoop to her."
> *Cœlum non animum muto dum trans mare curro.*
> Joannes Miltonius Anglus, Junii 10, 1639.

Here is John Bunyan's Bible with its worm-eaten cover and well-worn brass knobs, and here a book from Madame Pompadour's library, a dainty thing — bound with faded rose-colored watered silk, its cover chased in gold, illuminated with vividly tinted flowers and her royal coat of arms, meet memento of the imperious and intellectual mistress of Louis Fifteenth. Here is the original copy of Burns' "Scots wha hae wi' Wallace bled," in the clear bold writing of the poet, and here the original manuscript of Pope's "Essay on Man," with all the erasures and interlinings added by the fastidious writer, just as they were left by his pencil — O! how long ago at Twickenham — and here, lying with others on the library table in its plain morocco cover and soft ribbons, looking scarcely different from its mates, is a book once owned by the haughty and unfortunate Earl of Essex. What memories of passion and fury, of folly and fate, are recalled by these two little names written ages ago by their owner, Robert Essex?

Here are the manuscripts of Edmund Burke — letters written by his own hand, extending through a length of years, carefully bound. Great Britain has allowed to pass from her keeping these treasures of the great master of English eloquence, and they find a fitting shrine in the house of another master as great as he. In the same drawer there is a little old worn schoolbook, with a schoolboy's name written on the title-page in a schoolboy's scrawl, and with a schoolboy's spiral flourish at the end. The name is "JOHN DRYDEN;" and this little old book, the one that he used when at Westminster School, in 1646, is full of his Greek exercises, interlined throughout with Latin translations of the Greek sentences, in the boy's own hand. And the schoolboy's book of Old England of 1646 is the precise prototype of the schoolboy's book of New England in 1871.

Personally nothing could be more interesting than the first small printed copy of the "Spring" of Thomson's Seasons, published in 1728. This is the author's copy — the one he presented to the woman he loved. It was accompanied with the following verses, on the fly-leaf, written by his own hand: —

TO MISS YOUNG.

"Accept, loved Young! this tribute due
To tender Friendship, Love and you;
And with it take what breathed the whole —
Oh, take to thine the Poet's soul!

If Fancy here her power displays,
And if an heart exalts these Lays,
Thou fairest in that Fancy shine,
And all that heart is fondly thine."

On another page is copied a portion of a letter from Thomson to this lady, whom he was never permitted to marry. It has been said that model love-letters are rare in this nineteenth century. They may have been in the eighteenth; but in this it transmits to us, at least, one perfect. Its tender rhythm is not surpassed by the most melodious lines in the "Castle of Indolence."

"HAGLEY, *August* 29, 1743.

"At the source of this water composed of some pretty rills that purl beneath the roots of oaks there is as fine a retired seat as love could wish. There I often sit and with an exquisite mixture of pleasure and pain, of all that love can boast of excellent and tender, think of you. But why do I talk of sitting and thinking of you there? Wherever I am, however employed, I never cease to think of my loveliest

Miss Young. You are part of my being; you mix with all my thoughts, even the most studious, and without disturbing give them greater harmony and spirit. Ah, tell me, do I not, now and then, steal a tender thought from you? . . . . I would rather live in the loneliest corner of London with you than in the finest country retirement, and that too enlivened with the best of society — without you.

"Think with friendship and tenderness of him who with friendship and tenderness is all yours.

"JAMES THOMSON."

Even the doors of this room are hung with pictures. We pass by the "Gate of Victory" into the hall, which is covered with photographs, some many feet square, of the Coliseum, the group of St. Peters, and the Vatican, and other famous Roman and classical views. Beyond, the door opens upon the parlor — a small, lustrous *salon*, hung and carpeted in gold and azure, illuminated with mirrors and paintings, looking upon Lafayette Square — the lovely Nature without, complementing and crowning the lovely art within.

The house itself is a four-story brick dwelling, with Mansard roof; attractive by its cheerfulness more than anything else. A bright band of green grass holds it from the street, and visibly all that divides it from the Executive Mansion is the square, full of trees and birds and sunny children, which grow and rejoice between.

You have a glimpse of a small portion of Charles Sumner's home. Its chief charm lies in this, that it is the unique and beautiful expression of an individual nature. Everywhere it reveals the thought and feeling of its owner. No house can be a home unless in some sense this be true — unless its very furniture is imbued not only with the taste but the affection of its possessor. In Washington there are elegant and æsthetic houses; but, as a rule, the abodes of its public men are mere temporary stopping-places or great upholstered show-shops, showing little but the wealth or vulgarity of their owners. A material and commercial smartness is everywhere glaringly visible. This comes from the fact that mere speculators, schemers, and traffickers are so rapidly buying with money and patronage the high places of public trust, once filled by scholars, statesmen, and gentlemen.

It is impossible to recall the refined and scholarly memories of Jefferson, Madison, the two Adamses, Josiah Quincy, Edward Livingston, Edward Everett, and their peers, without regret. They were the men who brought the highest culture, the gentleness of gentlemanhood, combined with political acumen and power, to the administration of public affairs. The house just sketched is interesting as the home of a scholar and statesman, one of the last of that race of great scholars and statesmen so rapidly passing away.

VI.

GRAND DUKE ALEXIS IN NEW YORK.

"BROADWAY! Broadway is delicious!" said an English lady. "It is more intoxicating than Paris. Its very atmosphere is like new wine." All of us realize this at times. On an October morning, perhaps, when the sea-breezes flutter still in our garments, when the fragrance of the pine forests linger with us, and all the freshness that we caught amid the summer hills quickens our steps and blooms on our faces — then, stepping on its pavement, "Broadway is delicious." Looking down Broadway upon such a morning, reminds me always of Guido's "Aurora." Gazing up above the glittering walls into the exhilarating air, it seems as if one must see her coursers, with all the heralding graces, making their pathway to the sun. But no. The graces are all on the sidewalks; so, too, are the horses. Instead of spurning the clouds, they fall down on the cobble-stones, and are seized by the Society which takes care of horses and prepares them for the Kingdom of Heaven. Yet, with all the perils of its pavements, Broadway is delicious on an October morning. On such a morning we expected to see "ALEXIS." I came home from the country in season to see him; and, strange to tell, am not ashamed to own it. Most of my friends, I find, seem to feel that there is great merit in saying, "Oh! I didn't go *to see the Prince* — it was a mere happen;" or (with a superior air), "*I* don't run after princes." Well, I don't; but I like to look at them when they look as well as Alexis, and have a face and head so well worth studying as the pure type of an historical race. I went on to Broadway on purpose to see the son of the Emperor of Russia, and am more than obliged to Mr. Brady for the delightful seat in his gallery which gave that fair Romanoff face and magnificent head to the treasured pictures of memory. Every name outside of our personal life is what association makes it. Mere curiosity might lead a crowd to gaze at the Prince of Wales in Broadway; but to-day his name could inspire no enthusiasm. He has out-lived the fairest promise of his youth. His mother and poor Alexandra would shed a wife's and mother's tears for him; but it would be better for England to-day if he were dead. Eight centuries of kingly blood from William the Conqueror, through Robert Bruce, and all the lumpish and rakish Georges, may make him royal, but has failed to make him noble. If we made geese of ourselves over him to-day, it could only be for his mother's sake, or because he is heir to her crown. Her son Arthur Patrick aroused no enthusiasm in America. He was a very tame young man ; well enough, but no more. The most remarkable thing about him was his shirt-collar, and that was ugly. Royal blood, from William the Conqueror to Albert the Good, have failed to produce in him anything more than a perfectly common-place young gentleman. I never went into Broadway to behold him. It's a Prince I fancy, not princes. The Romanoff of the nineteenth century is a splendid creature. When the line of Ruric ceased, nearly three centuries since, the Romanoff came forth from the people, powerful and brutal, and made himself a king. Nearly three centuries have gone, and he is still a king — an absolute monarch over one of the largest empires of earth. To-day he is strong, chivalrous and gentle, stately and noble to behold. The young man Alexis comes from a race of giants. Peter the Great was a giant in frame as well as in mind. The Empresses Anne and Elizabeth were as strong as men. Catherine the Great, with the power and passions of a man, could strike a man down with one blow of her hand. The Emperor Nicholas, iron in muscle and will, was the handsomest man in Europe. His son Alexander, the present Emperor of Russia, is scarcely less remarkable for manly beauty, and in person and presence "every inch a king." The wife of Nicholas, beautiful and good, was a daughter of the almost divine Louisa of Prussia, the loveliest victim ever immolated to the cruelty of Napoleon the First. The present Empress of Russia comes from a princely house famous for the piety and graces of its daughters. Thus I said this young man Alexis, whose cortege will be here presently, inherits from his ancestors many of the most powerful, some of the worst, and some of the best traits in human nature. Meanwhile, through the crystal air came the distant throbbing of advancing drums and the measured beat of marching feet The last October day in its matchless procession of perfect days had gone by. It loitered long for his coming; but the ocean refused to give up Alexis. Now November had hushed her storms for a day, and hung out the brightest of blue banners to salute him. It is worth a journey to New York to see Broadway in all the bravery of an ovation. The daily repeated chill of long delay had failed to rob this of its splendor or majesty;

for in miles on miles of concentrated, eager human life there is always majesty. Far as the eye could see, up and down, Broadway was literally packed with human beings. Across the street, Stewart's shop of marble, covering an entire block, was lined at every window from base to summit with ladies and children. From the windows of other shops all goods had been taken, and, tier on tier, to their tops, they were lined with gayly-dressed women.

"Look there!" exclaimed one gentleman to another, in astonishment, at the sight of a great Broadway shop-window, filled to the top with feminine creatures. "That's the handsomest show-window I ever saw." The ladies blushed and looked discomfited at attracting such attention; but they would not come down. They would see the Prince. Men crowded the house-tops, clung to the walls and steeples of the churches; and one man (there is always sure to be one who must attract attention to his own insignificant self, no matter what the occasion) one man hung himself out from the spire of Grace Church, and amused himself by keeping humane mortals below in a perpetual fright lest he should drop upon the pavement and smash his foolish head. Flags flew from every house-top; pennons and devices floated out from ten thousand windows; boys stood on the street holding aloft garlands and baskets of flowers, from whose hearts stood forth in scarlet blossoms the name of "Alexis." Richly-dressed ladies, in open carriages, sat at all the corners. At last the crowd began to push forward, then to sway back before the advance of a platoon of mounted policemen. Then came more than a thousand policemen, in a solid body, as one man; then a regiment, with banners and band; then four regiments of young men, forming a hollow square. In its centre, in a carriage drawn by four jet-black horses, with gold-mounted harness, rode the young man of the hour. He sat head and shoulders above the three other gentlemen in the carriage, and was conspicuous, not for his attire, which was the uniform of a lieutenant in the Russian navy, but for his powerful stature, and for the height of his head, which rose like a dome under its "glory" of golden hair. People, thinking only of the prince a moment before, forgot him in admiration of the man. Handkerchiefs waved, huzzas went up. Alexis bowed his head to his friends. Thus, amid flowers and banners, beautiful women, glad music, and the shouts of the people, followed by miles on miles of mounted and marching men, thousands of whom were as fair, as young, and as brave as himself, the son of the Emperor of Russia entered the metropolis of the country to which he has proved so devoted an ally. For, after all, until the moment that they saw his face, it was only the son of the Emperor of Russia that the people waited to see. He was not even the heir to its throne. True, it had been told of him that his twenty-two years had already compassed deeds of heroism; that he was a true sailor in a storm at twelve years of age; that he had rushed into the water and saved a strange young girl from drowning, at the risk of his life; and these deeds proved that he was more than a prince — a man, with the inborn nobility of manhood in him. Yet not for this was he honored. He was welcomed for his father, who received an American admiral with royal honor, who has never spared money or pains, even in his reception of private American citizens, and who was America's steadfast friend in her darkest hour. It was New York welcoming Russia. Yet no less the Archduke Alexis wins good-will for himself wherever he goes. His striking person and presence, combined with a singular modesty of demeanor, disarms criticism, and inclines the loudest "sovereign" citizen to pardon him for having been born a prince, and to like him as a man. For this, personally, he will be the longest remembered and admired — that, had he not been the son of an emperor, no less he would have commanded respect and admiration as a man.

The Archduke Alexis is over six feet high, with great breadth and depth of chest, an erect carriage, and a head remarkable for its height and development of reverence, veneration, and benevolence. Whatever else he may forget to do, he will never forget to say his prayers. The upper part of his face is of remarkable beauty. The hair, waving and golden, is cut short. His forehead is intellectual, his eyes of deep blue, large and full, with those swift scintillations of everchanging expression which betray the soul and make the finest charm of any human face. The best of his face is its manliness. It is a thoughtful, earnest face, the face of a man who would be no less noble in trial and adversity than amid all the splendors of fortune. His hands are simply huge, and have the grip of a Polar bear. At least, they are capable of bearing more handshaking than ordinary hands. I saw him go through with this American ordeal the other evening. He did it with patience and grace, if not with enthusiasm. It gave a sturdy, unsentimental grasp to the daintiest kid-gloved hand outstretched to him. But the face of Alexis told many stories during the process. One instant it looked pleased, the next weary, the next indifferent, and the next would brighten again. "He is very handsome and agreeable," said a young lady who danced with him; "but he has the ugliest hand I ever saw." And, if she makes the thin, sensitive, nervous American hand her criterion, it is not strange that she calls this giant fist ugly. It is an ugly, honest hand, that looks as if it had travelled down the Romanoff line from a day when the Romanoffs were not "royal." If the Grand Duke can't dance well, he can walk with a will. Head and shoulders above all the company, he went about with Miss —— on his arm. The young lady was very graceful and pretty, in blue crape, with a little blue feather and pink *aigrette* in her hair. As the two went laughing and chatting through the crowd, they were fair to see. It was the story, old as the earth, of the youth and the maiden. In their glorious young manhood and womanhood both were royal. We prose over the vanity of earthly honors; yet no less it is the splendor of life to be born to its purple. It is of heaven to be young, beautiful, and beloved. "I was young *then*," Madame De Staël would say, and burst in tears, whenever, in exile or sorrow, she recalled the glory of her youth. If it is the scion of an illustrious race, the representative of a vast and friendly power, the son of an emperor, no less it is youth, beauty, bravery, and manhood, whom America welcomed in the young man Alexis.

VII.

A RAINY MORNING IN THE COUNTRY.

A RAINY morning in an old country home is rich in compensations. Only in the country do the real homes of the land remain unprofaned and unmolested. The great city is full of "residences," which change inmates every year. Occupied by nomadic and transitory tribes, precious memories and life-long associations have no time to take root within their shallow walls. They are merely stopping-places, in which hundreds of successive families halt for a season in their pilgrimage from the cradle to the grave. They are prized according to their rent, their modern conveniences, the fashion of the street on which they stand. The old home in the country is beloved because in it children were born and died; because in its old rooms sons and daughters have grown from childhood to man's and woman's estate; because its doors have closed behind them when they went forth to meet their fate, and opened in tender welcome when they returned in sorrow or in triumph from the world. What if its ceilings are low, its rooms old-fashioned, its antique furniture glossy with time instead of veneering: here Jenny was born, here Johnny died, here Tom and Molly were married, here father and mother grew old, and hither children and grandchildren came to renew the youth and revive the joy of the generation before. The old house is dear because it is a home consecrated to a family life, sanctified by all its love and suffering, by grief outlived and by affection perpetually renewed.

A rainy morning in such a house is a precious season. To be sure the old rooster in the barn-yard looks forlorn, and I am glad of it. His tail is very wet and droopy, and he waves that baton of power with a shade less of authority, and reminds me less aggravatingly than usual of Brigham Young, the only man on earth whom I really wish to be hung. The rain dims the jeweled leaves of the maples across the street. The sunshine, that sent a thousand glittering lances through their scarlet and amber masses yesterday, to-day has disappeared; the mountains have merged into a sky of cloud; the rain beats on the near roof in myriad pulses, which seem to keep time with the memories that fill this old closet. It is an old closet, full of old books — the family books of one, two, three generations. Here are the children's books — painted, scrawled, thumbed, and old. The children who laid them down are men and women now. And one, the little girl who died, is "a fair maiden in her Father's mansions." The boy who brooded for hours over the ballad of "Lucy Gray," and whose childhood was filled with mournful conjectures concerning her uncertain fate as stated in the closing verse in the "Third Class Reader," —

"Yet some maintain that to this day
She is a living child," —

has lived to grow sick and sad over human carnage, and to restore many a "solitary child." And the boy who painted his young "trainers" such a deep blue, while he read,

"Oh! were you ne'er a school boy,
And did you never train?"

lived to more then "play march, march away," and to face death bravely in many of his country's battles. Well, well, who would not be a child again, if only to be drilled in the "Rhetorical Reader," and to feel the new thrill when reading for the first time the "Burial of Sir John Moore," and

"On Linden, when the sun was low,"

with the real quiver of the "rising and falling inflection," and the exquisite pleasure of growing pathetic over the quaver in one's own voice, to say nothing of the delicious tears at the first consciousness of pathetic sentiment.

But, if one wants to note the varying fashion in mere literary style, let me commend them to the old magazines and annuals of vanished generations. Here is an old "Museum," published before I was born. Its front page is garnished with a full-length portrait of Washington Irving, in a frock-coat nearly to his ankles, boots with pointed toes, one thumb to his chin, a seal in the fingers of one hand, and a letter in the fingers of the other. A more affected and absurd picture of a sensible man it would be difficult to imagine. Yet it does not equal the description of it, copied from "Fraser's Magazine." It says: —

"From his steadfast gaze, and the smile of soft delight which is lighting up his countenance, we should think that he is thinking of the *fair clime of Andalusia,* and of the *dark blue waters of the Guadalquiver.* We know not if he be a *smoker;* but, to *judge* by his *gentlemanly appearance he ought to be one!* Smoking is and always has been a healthy and fashionable *English* custom. There were schools and professors established here for the purpose of teaching the mystery of smoking, on the introduction of the Virginia weed; and the mode of *expilficating* the smoke out of one's mouth is at present a shibboleth demonstrative of an English gentleman. We could hardly conceive of anything in the shape of a gentlemanly biped coming from the nondescript savages of America. We were, however, agreeably surprised in Mr. Irving, who, from a nine days' wonder, has become the greatest favorite," etc.

Touching the present day, and yet not of it, are Mrs. Lydia Maria Child's "Letters from New York." They are, as all letters should be, a reflection of their writer; and being this, are full of the sunshine of a sunny temperament, and the love of God and man and Nature. Indeed, a denizen of to-day must marvel how through any mere letters from New York could be filtered so much of the fragrance and bloom of field and wood, — so much of the light which hovers over sea and shore. It proves not only that to the heart that loves her Nature is never wholly absent, even in the great city into which she peers down between high housetops and through scanty patches of barren land; but also how since that day the great city has grown, feeding upon Nature and hiding her from sight. It reads like a romance to-day, these words written in 1844: "Wandering over the fields between Hoboken and Weehawken, I came upon the loveliest little clump of violets, nestling in the hollow of an old moss-grown stump." Alas! where that "loveliest clump of violets nestled" stone cellars strike far downward to-day, and high walls pierce upward, shutting humanity and its necessary vegetables in, and Nature and violets wholly out.

To one who never saw Brooklyn, Jersey City, Hoboken, save as blistering cities, it seems like a story-book to read of them all in these glowing pages as Elysian Fields, fringing and fanning with vernal beauty and delicious breezes great New York. It is harsh and hard, the inexorable law of growth in a vast city, which, in proportion to the advance of commerce and wealth, shuts Nature out. With all its splendor and resistless life, New York is fast becoming one of the loneliest places on the earth for a home. In its aggregate it is great and grand; in its individual life it is isolated and alone. The largest individual circle in it widens out but a little way. The sweetest, truest, greatest heart that throbs within its limit can cease to beat, nor yet be missed. One of the loneliest sights on earth is a funeral in Broadway. Year by year the resistless tide of change sweeps on, tearing up and bearing on human sympathies and landmarks with it. Where fountains played, and shade trees swung their protecting branches, and homes were sheltered a year ago, to-day shop-signs are thrust out, and the great palaces of trade push their heads high in air, and the human crowds jostling below are more and more strangers to each other. The days when Peter Stuyvesant stumped about on his wooden leg, and the Dutch burgomasters and their families visited from "stoop" to "stoop," through all the evening hours, are remote enough to belong to another world. "All, all are gone, the old familiar places." But it is comforting to learn that the growth of the city is not exclusively in houses, railroads, and bridges.

At least, we are better to the dogs than they were when dear Mrs. Child wrote her letters from New York. She says: "Twelve or fifteen hundred of these animals have been killed this summer. The manner of it strikes me as exceedingly cruel and demoralizing. The poor creatures are knocked down on the pavement and beat to death. Sometimes they are horribly mained, and run howling and limping away. The company of dog-killers themselves are a frightful sight, with their bloody clubs and spattered garments." Though further apart, after all, let us be grateful that we live in the era of Mr. Bergh and of the "Society for Prevention of Cruelty to Animals."

Here is a venerable book, belonging to a woman's library in a secluded New England village, unknown of railroads forty years ago. The staple of ladies' libraries in our day being composed of very "light literature" and sensational novels of the frothiest description, it is of interest to find out what sort of books our grandmothers — the women who spun and wove their own garments — read. This is one of them: "The Life of Mrs. Elizabeth Carter," of England. Oh, *what* a book for a rainy day! It transports me from my little closet of mouldy books to the own room of this great woman scholar of the eighteenth century, immediately after breakfast, when she says: "My first care is to water the pinks and roses which are stuck in about twenty different parts of my room."

Besides, though contrary to constitutional habit, I attempt to join her in her walks *before* breakfast; "sometimes on an open common, then in the middle of a corn-field, then in a close shady lane, never before frequented by any animal but birds. Then she naively adds: "When some civil swains pull off their hats, and I hear them signifying that *I* am Parson Carter's daughter, I had much rather be accosted with, 'Good-morrow, sweetheart;' or, 'Are you walking for a wager?'" This Parson

Carter did a very sensible thing. He educated his children himself — his daughters as extensively and thoroughly as his sons. He was rewarded. His daughter Elizabeth was the delight of his life and the comfort and support of his old age. When, through a decline of his health and spirits, he felt unequal to undertaking the education of his youngest son, the arduous task was assumed by his daughter. Though eagerly sought by the most learned and brilliant society of London, she resisted all importunities, and secluded herself in the country for five years, in order to fulfill this work. Yet, meanwhile, in her leisure hours she found time to translate "Epictetus," a work which made her known to the whole world of scholars. It was of this book that the Archbishop of Canterbury afterward remarked to her: "Here, Madam Carter, see how ill I am used by the world. Here are my sermons selling at half price; while your 'Epictetus' truly is not to be had under eighteen shillings — only three shillings less than the original subscription."

It was at the urgent request of the Archbishop of Canterbury and Bishop of Oxford that she at last reluctantly undertook this work. In reply to a letter asking her to write the life of Epictetus, she wrote to her friend, Miss Talbot,

1755: "Whoever that somebody or other is to write the life of Epictetus, seeing I have a *dozen shirts to make*, I do opine, dear Miss Talbot, that it cannot be I."

In 1756 her brother and pupil passed a triumphant examination and entered at Cambridge. Her biographer says: "Mr. Henry Carter is, perhaps, the only instance of a student at Cambridge who was indebted for his previous education wholly to one of the other sex; and this circumstance excited no small surprise there, when, after his examination, it was asked at what school he had been brought up."

In his extreme old age, her father became wholly dependent upon her for personal care. In reply to commiserating friends, she then wrote: "I am much obliged to you for the kind partiality which makes you regret my giving up my time to domestic economy. As to anything of this kind hurting the dignity of my head, I have no idea of it, even if the head were of much more consequence than I feel it to be. *The true post of honor* consists in the discharge of those duties, whatever they happen to be, which arise from that situation in which Providence has fixed, and which we may be assured is the very situation best calculated for our virtue and happiness."

I confess to a spontaneous liking for this learned and gentle lady of the eighteenth century. There is a charm in her sunny quietness that rests one in this noisy day. She studied and mastered Greek and many other languages without ado. She translated Epictetus in a manner which commanded the praise of the greatest scholars in Europe; but, *therefore*, did not disdain to make her father's shirts. The sewing-machine makes it superfluous that any woman should stitch her eyes out in our generation; but the disposition, come to be deemed almost a virtue, which scorns any labor of the hands because it is labor, which turns with contempt from the pleasant household tasks which for so many centuries have been preëminently woman's, calling that drudgery which adds so much to the charm of home, is a repelling drawback to the finest of modern accomplishments.

VIII.

MARGARET FULLER OSSOLI.

THE FRIEND.

Not a generation has passed since the remorseless waves of the ocean swept Margaret Fuller Ossoli from human sight, and already she wears the lustre of the historic woman. This is remarkable for an American; more remarkable that this American is a woman. We have our full share of men-heroes — heroes whose deeds have made them worthy of the Olympian days; but the women whom we have lauded the loudest have been essentially humdrum. Martha Washington was well enough. She knitted stockings well and loved her husband. Thousands of other women have done the same, whose pictures do not hang in our parlors or line our photograph albums. The women who, by virtue of high endowment, would have made their names immortal through lack of the mere chance of personal development, have died and made no sign; while the women whom we have most delighted to honor have been chiefly remarkable because they bore their husbands' names. But the name of Margaret Fuller is still spoken by those who knew her in life with an enthusiam, a reverence, a tenderness, which but few human beings inspire; and for which, amid the fragments of her recorded thoughts, we search in vain for a commensurate cause. She wrote suggestively and well. On every page we see the results of a wide and accurate scholarship, such as at that time no other American woman, and but few American men, had attained; yet in her there existed more than ordinary antagonism between thought and its slow instrument of expression, the pen. Her swift and ductile mind constantly outflew its halting paces. On her written page we continually feel her limitations. Her style is often involved, as if it stumbled for lack of room amid its own crowd of treasures. It is only occasionally, and that when she is writing heart to heart to a friend, that her expression seems to reach the utmost measure of her thoughts. Perhaps in her work on Italy, written after she had grown on through the deepest human experience, she attained to perfect freedom and power in the use of written language. But this perfect flower of her mind and heart perished with her. Thus in the fragmentary thought which she has left we find nothing adequate to her reputation. This makes her wide and ever-widening fame the more remarkable. It is another illustration of the illimitable power of one great personality. It proves how one rare individual, through the pure force of its individuality, may live on and on long after its human home has perished. In looking back through the centuries, we find that the fame of women has always been more purely personal than that of men. Men have perpetuated their names through their works and deeds; women, restrained in the use of their powers, have been able to leave little more to the world than the legacy of their lives. But to these lives the human race will never cease to pay homage. Thus Margaret Fuller never wrote anything that was half as noble as herself. There was a pathetic charm in her nature beyond the reach of her words; yet her words were often pathetic, and in oral speech were most eloquent. Her dear friend, James Freeman Clarke, says: "She did many things well, but nothing so well as she talked. For some reason or other, she could never deliver herself in print as she did with her lips. Her conversation I have seldom heard equaled. Though remarkably fluent and select, it was neither fluency, nor choice diction, nor wit, nor sentiment that gave it its peculiar power; but accuracy of statement, keen discrimination, and a certain weight of judgment, which contrasted strongly and charmingly with the youth and sex of the speaker. Her speech, though finished and true as the most deliberate rhetoric of the pen, had always an air of spontaneity which made it seem the grace of the moment." Had her powers taken their free course, she would have been an orator in her own way, taking multitudes captive by the wonder of her thought and the music of her speech. Never in the remotest manner affecting the tones or the gestures of men, this woman would have used the transcendent gifts which God had bestowed upon her as He had given them to her. She herself says: "If I were a man, the gift I would choose would be that of eloquence. That power of forcing the vital currents of thousands of human hearts into *one* current, by the constrained power of that most delicate instrument, the voice, is so intense —yes, I would prefer it to a more extensive fame, a more permanent influence." Not a man, she was no less eloquent. But her great gift, forced back upon herself, flowed out in full force only to her friends. We are conscious of its reflex power in her most familiar notes. In her more labored works we rarely feel a thrill of the real inspirational eloquence which pervades all her personal letters. Here we are constantly surprised by her exhaustive culture, by her wealth of illustration, by her almost universal comprehensiveness of intellect, by the warmth of her temperament, by the tenderness of her heart. What could not such a soul give to other souls, to whom she was allied by consanguinity of purpose, of pursuit, and of affection? Had she left no other record, that of Margaret Fuller as a friend would have been sufficient to have perpetuated her memory. She had a genius for friendship. Universal sympathy with human nature was one of her most prevailing characteristics. Her magnanimity, her large intelligence, her tenderness made her not only comprehend, but feel for every struggle of a human heart. Her subtle, penetrating insight pierced to the core of every being she met; thus she knew not only what it was, but what it might be. She saw the sleeping germ of beauty as well as of evil, and her mission to every nature was to give to it the best ideal of itself. There was no soul so lonely or abject that she did not feel drawn toward it through the virtue of its humanity. She was the beloved friend of the little child, of the aged, of the sick and of the poor. But as the cherished associate and equal friend of many of the leading thinkers of her country and time, Margaret Fuller's friendships assume more than a personal significance. They give to the world another illustration of that illustrious race of friendships between men and women of the highest type which in every age have been deeper, broader, and purer than the time in which they existed. These friendships illustrate also a still more significant fact in human history — viz.: that, despite the depravity which has characterized the average dealings of men toward women, even in the most depraved and bigoted ages, the higher order of men and women met in absolute individual equality; and that the personal power of the femininely grand woman in herself has always been more powerful than tradition, prejudice, or custom. Monica and St. Augustine; Susannah, and John, and Charles Wesley — friends no less than mother and sons; Francis de Sales and Madame De Chantal; Fénelon and Madame Guyon; Madame Swetchine and Lacordaire; Eugenie and Maurice de Guerin; Madame Roland and the Girondists; Hannah More and her masculine contemporaries, — all illustrate a type of friendships between men and women which has done all that a human relation could do to exalt human nature and to embellish human life. For love, the most powerful passion of humanity, is only exalted when it is born of friendship. The lover must be first and always the friend to be worthy to be the lover. To revere and love the individual, the personal essence which in its intrinsic quality separates the beloved being from every other in the universe, is the only love which survives all time and change. It is the only love which outlives beauty and youth. It made even Abelard and Heloise friends long after they had ceased to be lovers. The charm to inspire it in man lives only in the rarest woman. It made the soul of Madame Recamier more beautiful than her face, and her face was among the most beautiful in the world. It made all her hopeless lovers live and die her friends. It makes the picture of herself and Chateaubriand, sitting by the same fireside in their last days, one of the most attractive in the history of human affection. The splendor of his power, the passion of his intellect were gone; so too were the grace and glory of her youth. He was decrepit, she was blind, and both were old. They had outlived their friends, outlived everything which had once made their lives resplendent. The affection of their hearts, the friendship of their souls, surviving youth and passion, beauty and power, alone remained unshaken and unchanged. We pity the nature incapable of believing in this perfect friendship existing between man and woman. We find many such to pity. The majority of people talk as if there were but two extremes of relation which woman can sustain to man. She must be a pretty, tricky, artful creature, beguiling him of his reason, taking him captive through his senses, the panderer to his pleasures, at once his tyrant and his slave; or she must arm herself against him, accuse him, abuse him, as at once the sole author of her wrongs, the source of all her miseries. The fair, open land between, — the serene and sacred land of friendship, wherein men and women may meet in human sympathy, in kindred pursuits, in wide thoughts, and in beneficent action, — we hear constantly spoken of as a debatable if not impossible meeting-ground. It doubtless is, for the people who express this opinion; but never has been and never will be to those men and women who recognize and revere in each other the equal human nature which each alike receives from God. Always man needs woman for his friend. He needs her clearer vision, her subtler insight, her swifter thought, her winged soul, her pure and tender heart. Always woman needs man to be her friend. She needs the vigor of his purpose, the ardor of his will, his calmer judgment, his braver force of action, his reverence, and his devotion. Thus the mystic bond of sex which binds one half the matter and spirit of the universe in counterpart and balance to the other, gives even to the friendship of man and woman its finest charm, enabling each only through the other to preserve the perfect equipoise of intellect and soul. Such a friend was Margaret Fuller to the men who still speak her name with reverent tenderness. To have been at once a personal impulse, an intellectual inspiration in the lives of such men as Freeman Clarke, Hedge, Alcott, Channing, Emerson, George Ripley, Horace Greeley, Mazzini, was as high an individual privilege as ever came to an American woman. As the friend and helper of these men, her name will live associated with the most marked revolution in culture and ideas of her country and era. Without subscribing to their tenets, to be just, we must own that the transcendentalists of New England have given a keener impulse to thought (even in channels opposite to their own), a wider direction to personal culture, and a higher exaltation to personal character than has been given in the same period by any other body of scholars and thinkers in America. And when their history is dispassionately written, as it will be some day, the central figure amid this group of large-brained men will be this large-brained and still larger hearted woman. William Henry Channing says of her: "Of this body she was a member by grace of Nature. Her romantic freshness of heart, her craving for the truth, her discipline in German schools had given definite form and tendency to her idealism. On the other hand, very strong common sense saved her from being visionary, while she was too well read as a scholar to be caught by conceits, and had been too sternly tried by sorrow to fall into fanciful effeminacy. Men — her superiors in years, fame, and social position — treated her with the frankness due from equal to equal, not with the half-condescending deference with which scholars are wont to adapt themselves to women. They prized her verdict, respected her criticism, feared her rebuke, and looked to her as an umpire. Very observable was it, also, how with her they seemed to glow and brighten into their best mood, and poured out in full measure what they had but scantily hinted at in the circle at large. In these conversations she blended in closest union and swift interplay feminine receptiveness with masculine energy. She was at once impressible and creative, impulsive and deliberate, pliant in sympathy, yet firmly self-centered, confidingly responsive, while commanding in originality. By the vivid intensity of her conceptions she brought out in those around her their own consciousness, and by the glowing vigor of her intellect roused into action their torpid powers. She lived herself with such concentrated force in moments, that she was always effulgent with thought and affection. · So tender was her affection that, like a guardian genius, she made her friends' souls her own and identified herself with their fortunes." In closing his account of her life at Jamaica Plain, this same beloved friend, who had known her intimately from childhood, offers her as high a tribute as man ever paid to the friendship of woman: "The very thought of her roused manliness to emulate the vigorous freedom with which one was assured that, wherever placed, she was that instant acting, and the mere mention of her name was an inspiration of magnanimity and faithfulness and truth."

THE WRITER.

Margaret Fuller's written use of language was only limited when compared with her comprehensive thought and eloquence of oral speech. When she used language to illustrate her scholarship she was its master. Her intellect was widely and keenly critical; it traversed and measured universal life, equally the life of thought and the life of human experience. What she said of Goethe is preëminently true of herself. "She could see all that others live," but then she felt it also. When we remember that she brought this wide vision, this almost limitless culture, with all their opulence of suggestion and of illustration, to bear upon every character and work that she studied, we cease to wonder that in every critical line which she has left we perceive the touch of a master. In what language can be found another criticism of Goethe at once so intuitive, comprehensive, and critical, as hers, when judged by the severest standard of art? It is neither a eulogy nor a rhapsody; it is an exhaustive analysis. She measured not only his art, but the soul of his art; not his work alone, but the many-sided being of its author. She gives us the whole of Goethe's character in a single sentence: "Naturally of a deep mind and shallow heart, he felt the sway of the affections enough to appreciate their workings in other men, but never enough to receive their regenerating influence." And again: "Of Goethe, as of other natures where the intellect is too much developed in proportion to the moral nature, it is difficult to speak without seeming narrow, blind, and impertinent. For such men *see* all that others live; and, if you feel the want of a faculty in them, it is hard to say that they have it not, lest next moment they puzzle you by some indications of it. Yet they are not, *know* not; they only discern." Again: "Faust contains the great idea of his life; as, indeed, there is but one great poetic idea possible to man — the progress of the soul through the various forms of existence." After a subtle analysis of each of his various works, in the last paragraph of this superb criticism she utters these last words for Goethe: "Let us, not in surveying his works and life, abide with him *too much in the suburbs and outskirts of himself.* Let us enter into his higher tendency, thank him for such angels as Iphigenia, whose simple truth mocks at all his wise Beschrankungen."

The fields of critical literature offer rich harvests to the intellect of women. To those endowed with the power of comparison and of analysis, rather than the creative faculty, the largest opportunity waits. The printing-presses of the world throw off the embodied thought of the age faster than it can be read, faster than keen and accurately-balanced brains can weigh and judge between the chaff and the grain. Where in Margaret Fuller's time there was critical labor for one thoroughly-trained analytic mind there is now the labor and necessity for hundreds. But the extensive culture, the thorough mental discipline which enabled Margaret Fuller to command a leading position as critic of the greatest thinkers of the world, is just the discipline which the majority even of our most gifted women lack. It is not the want of native power, nor the want of opportunity, nor the envious prejudice of men, which debars women from the places of personal independence and influence which they covet, so much as it is their own lack of accurate knowledge, of faculties disciplined to special uses. One born with the faculty divine may write rhymes and romance, if one only knows the alphabet; one may do no small amount of showy and shammy work with just a smattering of lore; one may play brilliantly with things in general, without knowing anything in particular; but there is a vantage ground of thought as well as of action, which no mere show can reach, before which all shams fail. In the highest degree to weigh, measure, compare, analyze, and judge, involves not only the natural power to do it, but a long discipline and preparation of that power for its finest use. The total lack of such discipline is the most distinguished fact in the average education of women. The numbers and names of their studies are appalling. They know a little of many things — nothing accurately or thoroughly. How many women, called accomplished, who, if orphaned or widowed, are totally unable to earn a livelihood by instructing others in any branch of knowledge which they have been superficially taught. They are sure of nothing that they have studied. They possess no knowledge which they can make available; not a single power trained to use, not a mental gift which can command in gold an equivalent for its service. Thus through their very training inferior men are constantly taking the precedence of superior women. However little a man may know, he is usually sure of what he does know. His power, if limited, is at least available; and for success it is better to be able to do one thing perfectly than a thousand indifferently. How many bright women we know who are earning their bread in subordinate or menial positions solely through the want of the mental training which, did they possess it, would bear them at once to higher and better places. How many dull men we know full of authority, influence, and money, solely because their rather scanty powers were trained to special use; because they used them steadfastly for a definite purpose. Positions of responsibility and influence are constantly opening to women who are fitted to fill them. A few men may be envious and jealous about it — that is human nature; but even now there is nothing in their envy or jealousy which can prevent a woman from commanding the position which she has fitted herself honorably to fill. Then would it not be more effective if the leaders who devote themselves to the interests of women should spend a little less time in lecturing men, and a good deal more in the special training of their daughters? It is too late to atone for the superficial education or the lack of education in the women of the present generation, who are already weighted with all the burdens of mature life. But it is *the* hour to train the woman of the coming generation; to educate her for the largest use of her faculties; to give her that special training, in whatever direction she shows the most talent, which will make her mistress of at least one of the arts of the world, which in any emergency will enable her to be a self-respecting, self-supporting being. Let her be trained as her brother is trained, with a reserved power to meet the vicissitudes of life. Then, if she escapes, she is but the richer; and, if not, she may rejoice no less in the exceeding great reward of faculties trained to noble service. For such we commend Margaret Fuller as the most illustrious example of scholarship in woman which our country has yet given the world. Not that we should not be sorry to see the girl of our period writing Latin poems at eight years of age, or digging out Greek roots before breakfast, or in any way teaching her brain at the expense of her digestion. This is not necessary. In Margaret Fuller's early days it was supposed that the head condescended to no relationship with the stomach. We know better. We know that there cannot be a healthy brain without a healthy stomach, and that physical culture must keep pace with all intellectual development. But the unthinking prejudice against high scholarship in woman has been, not that it injured her stomach, but that in some very unphysiological way it repressed her heart. Nonsense! A man may be a scholar or a thinker; he is no less manly, it don't hurt his heart. A woman because she studies and thinks is no less a human being; but the *more*, in the proportion which her whole nature grows. Thus Margaret Fuller, illustrious as scholar and thinker, is no less preëminent as a daughter, sister, wife, and mother. Her heart, as capacious as her mind, compassed the fullness and sweetness of every human relation. Thus in the double perfect meaning we hold up her name as that of the grand typical woman of our country and time.

IX.

A FRENCH JOURNALIST.

MADAME GUIZOT.

THE woman journalist is not the outgrowth of our own land and generation alone. In other times and countries women have been associated with the press who might have been illustrious had not prejudice forbidden it. That same prejudice robbed it of many others whose special gifts would have added lustre to its triumphs. It was the caste of sex which held these gifts within the narrow limit of personal correspondence ; even here, in at least two instances, they have grown to be a supreme inheritance to the realm of letters. Think what journalists Madame De Sevigne and Lady Mary Wortley Montague would have made ! The genius of the woman whose name is recorded above was of a much more severe and lofty type. Madame Guizot was the youngest of that sober school of moralists which began with La Rochefoucauld and La Bruyère, and which included Vauvenargues and Duclos. She was born Pauline de Meulons, in Paris, 1773. Her father was the receiver-general for the district of Paris and the possessor of a large fortune. Her mother was of an ancient family in Périgord, which had been represented in the Crusades. Amid affluence and the most refined surrounding the little Pauline grew up a delicate and thoughtful child. She was seven years younger than Madame De Staël; and the forcing and repressing process which distorted the mental and spiritual development of that highly-endowed woman in early youth were unknown to the childhood and girlhood of Pauline de Meulons. Also unknown to her were the precocious ambition for display and the unhealthy sensibility which marred the character and happiness of her more brilliant friend. In her extreme youth Pauline de Meulons felt the shock of the Revolution of '87 and '89. Its frightful spectacles shocked her sense of justice, saddened her heart, and destroyed her youth; while it quickened all her faculties, made more powerful a mind naturally strong, critical, incisive, sensitive, and distinctively keen in its perception of truth and its hatred of falsehood. In 1790 her father died in poverty. While surveying a fortune of millions lost in debt, and her own mother reduced to absolute want, her moral force and natural energy sprang to the rescue, and tears fell from her eyes when, for the first time in her life, it occurred to her that she might possess mental resources upon which she could draw to retrieve the one and support the other. She read slowly, she studied faithfully, she perfected herself in the use of the English language. To begin, she wrote a novel, of course. But truth, not fancy, was the essence of her intellectual quality. She was born with the faculty of acute, almost unerring observation. She was keenly sensitive to everything weak, absurd, or false. She had creative power; but it subserved her analytical and critical force. By natural endowment she was born a journalist.

In 1801, M. Suard established the "Publiciste." It discussed politics, religion, literature, and ideology, and was the keen foe of the "Journal des Débats." At first, through the friendship of M. Suard, the "Publiciste" was opened to Mlle. De Meulons. For nearly ten years she contributed to its columns regularly upon every topic within its range — ethics, society, literature, the drama, novels, etc. She even maintained sharp controversies with herself, under an assumed character, attacking and defending herself with great acumen upon many of the exciting themes which then agitated the leading intellects of France. The two volumes of her "Conseils de Morale" are composed almost exclusively of extracts made from these ten years' contributions. Of some of these Madame De Staël wrote to M. Suard: "Pray tell me if Mlle. De Meulons is the author of the fragment on Vauvenargues, on Thibet, the English, etc.? They so far transcend the ordinary efforts even of a gifted woman that I fancied I detected your hand in the composition."

Mlle. De Meulons herself, speaking of the logical faculty in Borleau, says: "In him it was a delicate, sensitive, irritable organ, wounded by a false sense, as a fine ear is wounded by a false note, and rising in its wrath the moment it received a shock;" and Sainte-Beuve adds: "This same vivacity and vigilance of reasoning Mlle. De Meulons displayed during the singularly active period of her journalistic career." Like Madame De Condorcet, Madame Roland, and many other celebrated French writers and thinkers of the eighteenth century, she reflected the Latin mind through a loving study of its masters. Sainte-Beuve says of her: "She had something in common with Seneca—she touched antiquity through the most modern of the ancients." Like Seneca, she delighted to present truth in the guise of paradox. She was great in aphorisms. Many of the most profound, which have given her moral counsels a permanent place in literature, were gathered like unwrought gems from a great mine of miscellaneous articles. The most precious and permanent were often found in some review of a silly novel or insipid play; but she left the mark of greatness upon everything that she touched. And it was not the one-sided greatness of mere mental power; it was greatness of character, as well. At twenty-five she found herself overwhelmed with domestic embarrassments. A fortune of several millions laid in ruins. Upon this, by her own unaided labors, she met all claims, reserving nothing for herself but freedom from debt, earning day by day her own support and her mother's. Through all these ten years she sowed the most precious seed of her thought and life — seed whose still-ripening harvest is not yet all gathered in — seed sown in humility, obscurity, and need, in the apparently ephemeral soil of a Parisian newspaper. Then, as to-day, the world did not lack croakers to decry a woman's work; nor the Job-friends, of whom all workers possess so many, who bemoan that, if you have gifts, you must "waste them on a newspaper." Above all this "venomous compassion" she rose, as every great woman should rise to-day, into a region of thought and action where it cannot touch her. She replied once, in her "Letter of a Female Journalist to a Friend," published December 18th, 1807: "My articles are censured, are they, my friend? That, of course, is to their credit; but you tell me the censure extends to me personally — to the stand I have taken as contributor to a journal, and especially as a critic of theatrical novelties. I am reproached, therefore, with being a woman, not surely with being a journalist; for those of my censors who know me know very well why I am that. But do they not fear that they may have wherewith to reproach themselves, if by words lightly uttered they succeed in destroying, or, at least, in rendering more difficult of exercise, the courage found requisite for the sacrifice to what I considered a duty of the conventionalities which my education and habits had taught me to respect. I know them, my friend, and so do you — these conventionalities, which make the *rôle* of a journalist the very oddest for a woman to choose, if, indeed, it ever were adopted from choice. It cannot, I assure you, appear as ridiculous to these friends of yours as to me; for they have never seen it so near. If they knew, as well as I, the grave interests at stake, the important considerations to be weighed, the absurd griefs to be consoled, and the still more absurd homage to be accepted; the buzz of petty passions, whose noise invades a woman's very solitude; and if they could see, amid all this, a work to be done without charm for the mind, or indemnification for the vanity, then they might say what they thought, and think, if they pleased, that I had undertaken this work for my own pleasure. But let them not attempt to pity me, for that would be as unreasonable as to blame."

One must pause before the simple dignity of these words, so penetrated with the ideas of duty and responsibility, as they recall the frivolous assertion so frequently and so flippantly made, that women enter every calling, especially that of journalism, without preparation, without forethought, without power, chiefly to gratify a "hankering after notoriety or public applause."

In 1807 Mlle. De Muelons, through fresh domestic misfortune and impaired health, was compelled to discontinue her journalistic labors for a season. At this time she received a letter written by an unknown hand, containing an offer from the writer to supply articles for the "Publiciste" in her place, which he would attempt to make worthy of her as long as her own were interrupted. After hesitation this offer was accepted. And for months M. Guizot — then very young and perfectly obscure — supplied to the "Publiciste" miscellaneous, dramatic, and literary criticisms in place of the ones that had made the journal illustrious under the signature of P. Thus the after great historian and statesman of France began his life of letters by doing the work of a woman, to him personally unknown, under her own signature. Personal acquaintance created a bond between these two, more powerful than age or conflicting opinion, lasting as life, and not dissolved in death. In 1812 they were married, and in mature life Pauline de Meulons begins a new career. The journalist is not lost, but merged in the completer woman. She was not defrauded of youth at last, though it came to her somewhat past its season, as it must to many. She who at twenty-five wrote with the wisdom of age, at thirty-nine wrote with the glow of youth warming every conviction. In the study of an intellectual woman nothing is more interesting than to trace the change wrought in her intellectual life and labor through the perfect development of her womanhood. In almost every instance it is sufficient to verify the belief that the great underlying motive force of the universe is that of sex. The greatest feminine writer can never be a woman who has stopped short of the complete fulfillment of womanhood. Thus, after more than ten years of intellectual work, which would have reflected lustre upon the greatest man, there came a time when the woman herself was greater than the utmost that she had ever done. As the grandest men are the most simple and childlike, so the grandest women are the most womanly. If by reason of intellectual power they are stronger than the mass, by so much are they more powerful in every attribute essentially feminine. The great man is never so great to us as when we feel his grandeur through the spontaneous revealing of a childlike soul; and an intellectual woman never so potent as when we feel the magnetism of her genius through the greatness of her heart. Thus of the illustrious woman whose public career is here so partially sketched it can truly be said that her latest years were her greatest. Under the stress of necessity her intellect flowered first; later, in the holy atmosphere of affection, her heart. In 1806 she wrote: "A woman who has reached the end of youth must not suppose that she has any further concern with passion — not even with vanquishing it. Her strength must henceforth lie in calm, and not in courage."

Six years later, when she had done with

youth, she loved and married a man intellectually and spiritually her peer. She lived to look into the face of her child; then life and the whole universe took on a value unknown before. She became the writer of a new age. The mother of a man, there dawned in her an absolute perception of harmony and duty, of faith and truth, of liberty and law, but dimly guessed at in her maidenhood. "Once a mother, she felt the necessity of believing in a better future and a perfectible humanity in the virtue of those generations that would be contemporary with her child." She wrote books for children, she espoused the labors and convictions of her eminent husband. She loved love, and she loved to live. She, calm reasoner, — looking into the face of husband and child, then into the face of death, — felt a yearning and a regret for which there was no speech. Into her last hours were gathered a passion and a pathos which youth never brought.

On the 1st of August, 1827, while her husband was reading to her a sermon of Bossuet, on the Immortality of the Soul, she passed from earth, and was buried, by her own desire, according to the rites of the Reformed Church, of which her husband was a member.

Sainte-Beuve says of her: "Thus died a

woman who has had no superior in our generation. The sentiment which she inspires is such as can only be expressed in terms of respectful admiration; such that it seems almost a sin against one who was always intent upon *being*, rather than *seeming*, to pronounce on her behalf the words *future* or *glory*."

X.

FANNY FERN.

SARA PAYSON WILLIS PARTON (Fanny Fern) died October 10th, 1872. Mr. Bonner, in the New York "Ledger," noticing her dangerous illness, which he said "will carry immeasurable sorrow to the hearts of our readers," added: "The following is the first article that Fanny Fern ever wrote for the 'Ledger.' It was published in the 'Ledger' of January 5th, 1856 — over sixteen years ago. Since that day she has never failed once to furnish an article for every number of the 'Ledger.' We think no other editor can say this of any contributor for the same period of time."

In 1851 Fanny Fern found herself a widow with two little girls clinging to her for support as well as care. In 1851 it must have been harder for a woman to suddenly find herself confronting the world, with only her brain and hands and loving heart between her and want. It is appalling enough now for any woman accustomed to life-long dependence to suddenly find all the responsibilities of bread-winning and household support devolving on her own unaided labor, although manifold opportunities for that labor were undreamed of twenty years ago. At that time the best educated of American women were educated for nothing in particular — unless to be school teachers, which, of course, created, at least, a dozen teachers for every school. But death and misfortune have ever been remorselessly indifferent to the fancies of the fastidious or to the prejudices of society. In the abstract, lovely is the theory that a woman should always be protected, always cared for. But all the same as if they were never uttered, every day death strikes down the protector, or fatal conditions put him forever beyond reach. Then, in the face of the finest theory, woe to the woman standing alone who cannot honorably take care of herself.

Fanny Fern, as a school girl in Catherine Beecher's seminary, in Hartford, tore the leaves out of her "Euclid" to curl her hair with. Hartford still holds traditions of her girlish escapades, tricks, and manners, but has preserved no record of her scholarship. In her way, she probably was about the same sort of scholar in the Hartford Seminary that Henry Ward Beecher was in Amherst College, — learning as little as possible from books, but everything from Nature, from human beings, from her own acute faculties, electrical temperament, and deep, passionate heart. What it was for such an one to find herself suddenly cast forth from a home of ease, a life of love and happiness — widowed and poor — no one may tell but she who has sat down amid the ashes of all earthly joy. To-day the world is not over-kind to lonely womanhood. Least of all is it to a womanhood so sharply defined in its originality or individuality that the very force of its innate quality pushes it out of the accustomed groove assigned to average womanhood. All that Fanny Fern suffered in those early days of womanhood, none but God and her own soul could ever know. It does not follow that her "friends," as worldly friends go, were basely cruel beyond their kind, if they did neglect, pass by, and slight the young widow — proud, independent, poor, who to them besides was probably erratic, hard to manage, and "queer." Nor does it prove that hers was a malicious nature, because under its first keen sense of neglect and injury, the passionate heart in its need, the proud spirit in its poverty, flung back in return resentment and defiance, bitterness and even hate. It was a transient disturbance. It was the stress of misfortune, the stirring of wrong, which wrought up the wrath of her nature. She tossed off the foam of her rage, leaving the pure wine below her, clear, bright, effervescing. Thus she poured it out in fullness and sweetness to the last.

Well, she did not want to go into a shop. She could not teach school and live by it; but she could write an essay that was yet a sketch — dancing, dashing, satirical, witty, human, pathetic — a sketch which in that day, at least, was a need in journalism; a sketch for which she alone in temperament and power had received the patent; a sketch which nobody else on earth could write but Fanny Fern. She wrote it. With poverty crouching on the hearth, with her little girls tugging at her skirts, with her fiery blood rushing through her veins, all freighted with love of love and hate of hate, she wrote it. Then she put it into a little satchel, and sallied forth to sell it. That must have been awful. There was a relief in writing it. What a delicious first vent it must have been for the flood-tide of wrath and love that came rushing after. But to go out to seek somebody else to find it precious — precious enough to pay money for it; to set a price on it; that heart-throb, to ask a price for it — that must have been awful. A man going from office to office to sell a poem or a leader must be a sorry sight. A woman compelled to peddle by voice and eye such a ware must be a sadder sight still. She endured many a supercilious glance, more than one rebuff, of course, on her weary round. A woman trying to sell her own composition from a bag, no doubt appeared childish to these men of affairs. The curly head, the little satchel, the little sketch, did not look the least like business. Beholding the three, what prophet of them all could foresee that the dainty reticule with its contents stood for *one hundred and thirty-two thousand* copies of a single book! She found an astute purchaser at last. He liked the sketch, took it, and paid her for it — fifty cents.

Its fresh fearlessness hit the "general reader;" its veining pathos touched ten thousand hearts. Fanny Fern had hit the right nail on the head; it was a golden one. She struck again and yet again, for twenty years — for sixteen years never missing a single week. She was fortunate in her publisher. Sagacious and practical, she selected one not for his own fame, who would consider it quite sufficient to stamp his name on its title-page, and leave her book to take its chance; but one whose reputation would, in a degree, depend upon her own. Already her "Fern Leaves" were scattered through the length of the land. People shrugged their shoulders; but all the more they read and bought. Critics said they were flippant, sarcastic, irreverent, masculine, and bitter. Nobody said they were lackadaisical, weak, or stupid. No matter what was said, all the more people bought them and read them. Of the first volume of "Fern Leaves" seventy thousand copies were sold in America. "Little Ferns for Fanny's Little Friends," sold sixty-two thousand in the United States, while forty-eight thousand copies were sold in England alone.

In touching child-life, as in nothing else, did Fanny Fern prove the depth and tenderness of her true womanhood. She might be unjust to men, satirical to women; but to a baby — no matter how sour or woebegone — she was never less than the mother. From first to last she was the championess of childhood. Not a torment, not a stomach-ache, not a delight could come to a child, or ever came to one, of which she has not taken cognizance. It has no possible right that she did not defend, no error that she did not tenderly forgive, no sorrow with which she did not sympathize. With children, so with mothers. Her own motherhood was the deepest and sweetest inspiration of her being. Through her own mother-life she felt that of all mothers. To the world at large Fanny Fern may be a fierce hater of shams, a brusque, masculine, and even naughty woman. To the mother who has watched her child sicken and die, who has buried the baby out of her bosom, and cut Fanny Fern's loving grief over just such a baby out of a newspaper, and hidden it in her work-basket — to this mother (and I see her in so many lonely homes) Fanny Fern is the most lovesome of all mortal beings.

Broadway has given me two pictures of this woman, which I shall always tenderly keep. One is of the winter of 1859-60. Each bright day one could see from afar that haughty head, with its wealth of golden curls, and that peerless step, which had in it a fine disdain, that I never saw equaled in woman. Always quietly and elegantly dressed, she was striking by force of her very presence. With strongly marked features, a noble figure, and elastic step, which yet carried with it the proud dignity of a queen, she could not fail to attract a second glance even from an unthinking stranger. On either side walked a fair young daughter. One, much taller than her mother, was especially noticeable for her wide blue eyes and long, fair curls. Within two or three years she married and died, leaving, as a dying gift to the mother whose heart was broken, a little child of her own.

In time Broadway gave another characteristic picture of Fanny Fern. In the bright autumnal afternoon she walked Broadway with the young daughter left, and the baby. Thus I saw it one day in its nurse's arms. The crowd wedged us all pat in a corner. Fanny Fern was talking with baby. Oblivious of all the world, she saw her kingdom in its eyes. Such a transfigured face, such baby talk! The direst Calvinist could not despair of the "final salvation" of a woman who could look and talk like that to a baby. It was of this child that she wrote privately: "Our little Effie has never been left with a servant; and, although to carry out such a plan has involved a sacrifice of much literary work, or its unsatisfactory incompleteness, I am not, and never shall be, sorry. *She* is my poem."

As a writer she never reached her own highest mark, never wrote up to the highest level of her powers. A passion for truth, a hatred of shams, a contempt for pretense, slashed with satire, sarcasm, humor, and wit, all electrified by an abounding vitality and an exuberant love of mischief and fun, marked every utterance which she committed to print. Yet scarcely less was everything that she wrote veined with a deep, loving pity for human nature, a delight in the natural world, of which she was a happy interpreter. One could not read the slighest sketch from her hand without being conscious that it came from a strong and honest heart, and from a head of unexhausted power. Yet the conditions under which she wrote, made it impossible that she should concentrate, elaborate, be continuously an artist, although in one form of utterance she was ever unapproached. It was her lot, as it is the lot of so many of the brave, bright, men and women of this generation, to serve her day, to meet the exigencies of the hour, to say the word that the present demanded without reference to the future. And she was true woman enough to recognize the fact, and to modulate her life upon it, that to *be* is higher than to say, even though your word be said in a form of the finest art; and that to mould an immortal soul is the divinest work that can come to woman or man.

This sketch is not written to invade the sanctity of private grief or to pronounce judgment upon its subject, either as woman or writer. It is only an unstudied tribute to a representative woman, who was one of the earliest to prove to American women that an honorable independence is within the reach of all who bring to bear upon any avocation to which they are adapted the industry, the faithfulness, the fearlesness, which characterized her; a word of tender regret for one whose bright exuberance of life it has ever seemed could never go out; a woman who, whatever her missteps were in struggling upward to its holiest standard, always, through all her days, loved the religion of Jesus Christ, and loved little children.

XI.

HORACE GREELEY AND EDWIN FORREST.

CERTAINLY no two men living were more thoroughly known in every phase of their being to their countrymen than were Horace Greeley and Edwin Forrest. Each in his own way perpetually published himself. Each in distinctive spheres of art illustrated the highest order of talent of its kind. Each exemplified in his daily walk and conversation opposing types of manhood. Each in dying illustrated the law of his whole existence. In death, the whole picture of each life was seen in epitome. In life, the success of each man was self-made This fact affected each man according to his nature. It made Mr. Greeley feel superior to all colleges, and to all that colleges could bestow. It made Mr. Forrest feel superior to all other men. Edwin Forrest loved a few men. Horace Greeley was devoted to mankind. Forrest applied all his vast energies to the delineation of art and the gratification of himself. Greeley performed gigantic labors in behalf of ideas, consumed without stint every faculty and power he possessed in the service of humanity. The centre of one man's life, of his love and longing and labor, was himself. The centre toward which the other tended, through all yearning and effort, was the upbuilding of human nature. This self-centralization and this superiority to self-gratification each man illustrated in every phase of his life and of himself. Nowhere was it seen more distinctively or contrastingly than in their social and domestic existence. Horace Greeley clung to his wife through all fates and trials. An organism too acutely strung to bear life's common ills without friction, peculiar theories of domestic economy, with prolonged years of ill health, made it impossible, at times, that she should make the home of her overladen husband all that he needed. There were years, and these the ones in which his toils pressed heaviest, when, through stress of circumstances, Mr. Greeley scarcely had a home. Some of his books were written amid discouragements and in discomfort which would have appalled and paralyzed any man less a Cato in his mould. Many homes, bright, genial, full of gentle hearts, opened to him; but they were not his own.

Women gifted, good, and beautiful trusted him, cared for him, and ministered in many ways to his weary life. No man could have felt more exquisitely than he the ministries of such souls. No woman ever was his personal friend, trusting him, caring for him, who was not helped by the word and deed of his companionship toward the truest and noblest womanhood. No praise higher than this can woman offer to the memory of man. His friendships were catholic, comprehensive, and abiding. They held within their steadfast range some of the most illustrious as well as some of the most purely and sweetly domestic women of his time. Amid these, while his wife afar vainly pursued the mirage of health, he stood, in fact, a homeless and solitary man. But he never faltered in his work. He never swerved in his allegiance. He loved one woman, was true to her. She was the wife of his youth and the mother of his children. When her last struggle came, as he said, "in the darkest hour;" when for thirty sleepless nights and days he watched the last earthly light go out in the lustrous eyes which had enchanted and enchained his heart for more than thirty years, he felt his own life wane with it; and when it had gone, he knew had gone also both his power and his desire to live.

In the fullness of his fame, in the prime of his powers, and in the flower of a masculine beauty rarely bestowed upon man, Edwin Forrest, while the lion of the most exclusive London society, married Catherine Norton Sinclair, an Englishwoman, famous also for her beauty and her gifts. The marriage predicted before he left America, begun with such cloudless auguries, ended in a disgrace and wretchedness never transcended. Husband and wife became unreconcilable foes. Yet all records bear witness that they begun their life in New York with every prospect of happiness. Their house was a centre of fashionable, literary, and artistic society. Perhaps they were not worthy of the rich estate to which they had been called, too unclean for the holy sacrament to which he was ordained sole priest and she sole priestess. One, at least, was. He had received sole homage so long he would not share it now — least of all with his wife. She attracted admiration on her own behalf. This he would not endure. Claiming and practicing all license himself, he demanded of her the virtue which he outraged. She may have been a sinner, or may not. I know nothing about it. But the world knows that the crimes of which he accused her had made his own life a shame. He accused his wife of the vice which had made his own career notorious, and then proceeded to punish her with ruthless cruelty which alienated from him forever the sympathies of the better portion of mankind. It was not because Edwin Forrest was separated, or even divorced from his wife, that made his after days so isolated; but because he never ceased to his last day to persecute with malignant cruelty the woman whom he had sworn that he would love and cherish. Had like punishment been meted to him according to his sins, what would have been his fate? It was his wife who procured the divorce, forfeiting none of her rights or honors; and from that hour he never devoted half the genius to the delineation of Shakespeare that he did to the subterfuges that he hoped would save him from the payment of her alimony. Thus it came to pass that for years and years he lived on in the great mansion in Philadelphia not only a solitary, but a desolate man. Amid more wealth than he could ever consume, amid books and statues and pictures — exquisite pictures of child-life — he was alone. In his home hung the picture of two little children; one bathing her naked feet in a brook — the other stepping out of it with the sunlight on her head. It is told of this man how for hours he would shut himself away, gazing upon this picture. He had wealth and fame and many honors. But no child bore his name like a crown. No child-voice rained its music through those lonely halls. No soul is so utterly alone as that one who nurses in silence and secret a solitary passion, be it of love or hate. Self-love and wife-hate, developed into brooding and abiding passions, separated Edwin Forrest from the brotherhood of man and the true fellowship of pure women. No person who ever heard him utter the tenderest passages of Othello, of Hamlet, or of Lear can doubt his latent capacity to feel the deepest and tenderest emotions of the human heart. He comprehended beauty, sweetness, goodness, at times even moral greatness. He loved pure and tender ideals; but not with the abiding love, with the overmastering force which could hold his stormy passions in abeyance. Yet this comprehension, this capacity made more keen in him the consciousness of all that he had missed and all that he had lost. They deepened his solitude. They gave intensity to his sense of isolation and to his misery. As he lived, so he died — alone. How the iron soul met the supreme messenger no soul may tell. There was no one to seek the silent chamber but a faithful servant. She waited long to hear the heavy step on the solitary stair; and when he came not, and she went to him, she found that he had already met his fate. While dressing, to begin the life of another day, the hand forgot its cunning, the haughty head bowed to its first and last conqueror, the soul of a master void of tender glance or loving farewell or reprieve of warning struck out into the unknown. What a contrast to the death hour of his great contemporary. Death had robbed him before, how keenly and closely. His dearest hope, his life-long love had passed before him within the vail. The final blow that smote him struck the heart of the nation. It paused to lament its friend. His foes forgot his foibles. His caricaturists spoke only of his virtues. The daughters who loved him to idolatry hung upon his dying breath, and the friend whose sacred affection had followed and served him for more than forty years received his last glance of recognition in tender farewell, as soul and body parted forever. "I know that my Redeemer liveth," was his first conscious exclamation as his soul came back from the eclipse which precluded its eternal morning. More than twenty years before, in the yearning of his first great grief, when "Pickie" died, he wrote: "Now all that deeply concerns me is the evidence that we shall live hereafter; and especially that we shall live with and know those we loved here." Through storm and conflict and wounds unprecedented, the divine assurance was his. He uttered it in the moments of final passage. Who may measure the sublime satisfaction, the utter content born of that divine verity, healer of all mortal wounds, last, best hope of immortality! We who live know how attractive and enchanting this world is. They who die alone are sure that for its broken promises there can be no fulfillment, no, nor recompense, save in the full fruitions of an hereafter.

Every human life teaches one supreme lesson. That of Edwin Forrest is that no man, no matter how vast his resources or endowments, is sufficient unto himself. While in the life and death of Horace Greeley we are made equally sure that the man who through his own being yet lives for mankind, whatever his weaknesses, will survive in the heart of the humanity which he served; and, whatever his defeats, that he will find in death his final recompense and finest triumph.

XII.

LOLA MONTEZ.

LOLA MONTEZ delivered her first lecture after her last return from Europe in Mozart Hall, New York City. Whether the story of Lola's conversion brought them together to see the "change," or if it were simply the magnetism of the brilliant and naughty countess herself, I'm sure I don't know, but a more refined and intelligent looking audience seldom greets a metropolitan lecturer. Lola appeared, looking as radiant as her beautiful portrait, hung out on Broadway, and quite as young. Those who expected to behold a *passé* woman, whom they had heard of ever since they were babies, a nervous skeleton of buried charms, were astonished to see her, on the brilliant rostrum of Mozart Hall, looking not a day more than twenty-five. This wonderful preservation of youth may be attributed to a young, elastic heart, which, in spite of time, the tear of travel, and a thousand tornadoes of passion, revels in a perpetual spring; but quite as likely owed some of its perfection to sundry pastes and powders, the famous receipts of which Lola published for the benefit of the whole civilized feminine world. The lithe grace of her form was displayed to advantage in its voluminous garb of black velvet; a lace collar encircled the throat; cobweb laces fell over the arms, and a pocket handkerchief of the same fascinating fabric, floated in one delicate hand. She wore no jewelry, not even a breastpin or ring, — a bouquet of natural flowers being her only ornament. In an æsthetic point of view, it was worth more than the admittance fee simply to look at so complete a specimen of nature and art, without once thinking that you saw in her the beautiful woman of the nineteenth century, whose name in coming history (whether justly or unjustly) will be coupled with those of Pompadour, De Maintenon and others of their class. But when the great blue eyes grew scintillant with smiles, and the electric voice in most exquisite intonations vibrated through the great hall in these words, — "I hope none of you will accuse me of abusing the English," every reputed sin of the speaker was forgotten, and the audience, unconsciously, yet perfectly, seemed to pass within the sphere of her control. Not an element of popularity was wanting in this lecture. Wit, satire, sarcasm double edged, yet sheathed in smiles ; history, politics, religion ; quotations from Scripture ; anecdotes of society, all followed each other in brilliant succession.

She mixed with her careless gossip a strange quantity of sagacious thought, and of earnest, humane reflection. Rarely a man, and very rarely a woman, holds so complete a control over the modulations of voice as did Lola. Ever changing, its intonations were perfect and sweet as they were infinite. In her physique ; in the perfect abandon of her manner ; in her voice, were hidden the secrets of her power. The rest was centered in her head, rather than in her heart. She had a most subtle perception of character, a crystal intellect, and any quantity of *sang froid.* The delicate skill with which she played upon that harp of many strings, a popular audience, proved her to be the natural diplomat. She carried the audience with her completely ; and when at last the velvet robe, the laces, the bouquet of flowers, and the rarely radiant face made their courtesying exit, it was amid the most enthusiastic and deafening applause.

. . . .

Poor Lola Montez is dead. The newspapers

gathered up the records of her death-struggle, and the strange incidents of her most eventful life, and made personal columns of the rarest interest. They can tell no more new tales of Lola. There will be no more erratic actions, no more eccentric freaks, no more wild exploits or doubtful liaisons to record of her. The beautiful *intrigante*, the clever diplomatist, the erring, willful, wayward woman, the generous and loving woman is dead. Her wondrous wit and beauty and brightness have gone out under the winter snow; and the last story is told, — " She died." If it must be any, may it be men who shall now prove accusing disciples with stones all ready to fling at her memory. Let women be kind, and grant at least the meed of a tear or a sigh for her, because she was a woman. In reading the lives of the world's famous women, — women who reigned in society, in literature, in politics, women whom men flattered, followed, worshipped, and obeyed, — nothing in all the splendor of their lives is so impressive as the story of its close. Of all the gorgeous women of the past, no matter how great their dower of genius, of beauty, or of power; the great Elizabeth, the courtly Maintenon, the glorious De Staël, all that can be said at last, is, " She died." And in dying, how did the fashion of this world fade from the once entranced vision; how did its paltry gauds slip from the loosed hands, and, at last, nothing could suffice within those wasted fingers, save the Bible and the cross. This story of life was repeated once more in all its wonderful significance when the minister of Christ found the most beautiful and gifted courtesan of the nineteenth century weeping over the story of the Magdalen. Lola Montez, who once ruled a kingdom and its king; whose palace-home was beautiful with all that wealth and art and love could lavish; who knew all the triumphs, the vicissitudes, the sorrow, which wonderful beauty and misdirected gifts can bring, had little more than enough to buy the narrow house which shelters her now in Greenwood, and that little more she bequeathed to the society which saves in its tender charity the outcast women of this city. "Baroness of Rosenthal," "Countess of Landsfelt," titles which she had once been proud to bear, she was equally willing to lay aside at the door of the grave; and "Eliza Gilbert," her maiden name, was the one which she chose to be recorded on her simple coffin. Lola Montez died poor, but not friendless; she was surrounded by many who loved her for the inherent sweetness of her nature; and it is much to say of any one, which was truly said of her, that those who knew her best loved her most entirely. If she was erratic, high-tempered, and irritable, she was also generous, forgiving, and affectionate. The result of the former infirmities have been published largely to the world; but the acts, born of the latter, her munificent charities, her deeds of ruth and mercy to the poor and sorrowing, she never blazoned; yet we may believe that they found a higher and purer record. In the main, the public journals dealt generously and justly with her memory. If they did not attempt to justify her faulty life, neither did they altogether forget the misfortunes which controlled that life, and which were sufficient to hide a multitude of sins more heinous than hers. The New York "Times," in its kind and truthful obituary, said "The sensation of helplessness which she had experienced, and the indignities to which it had subjected her, were the causes which first directed her attention to the subject of some profession in which she might attain an independence. The stage is the aspiration of all lorn womanhood, and towards the stage she turned her best endeavors." It is a very easy thing to denounce the life and character of another. No high qualities are demanded to judge as the world judges. But it takes a larger insight, a wider, saintlier charity to penetrate far back to the inevitable circumstances which gave color and shape to that character and life. All possibilities of goodness, as well as of evil, lie in the soundless depths of such a nature as Lola Montez. The atmosphere in which it is forced to grow decides which shall be warmed and sunned into blossoming, and which shall lie dormant forever. Think of this, mother, when you look into the burning eyes of the girl-child beside your hearth, whose fathomless soul you have never sounded, whose mysterious future you cannot foretell! Bless God, if you have grace to guard and guide her; left to herself and the world, what might *she* become?

XIII.

THINGS GONE BY.

THE cottage on Fourth Street is closed, and its gate is fastened. I lean against its fence, and try to make its trees and flowers seem as they did one year ago. There is not a shrub nor flower here that was not planted by a single pair of hands; not a plant but was loved by one human heart. I try to bring that woman back and make her real again. In no other human being had I ever seen quite such intensity, such tenacity of life, such wide-reaching, irrepressible sympathies, such boundless benevolence. How many wounds she bound up, how many dying soldiers she nursed and cherished, how many toilsome journeys she took, how many sleepless nights she passed for their sakes. Yet how many of all who received life anew from her hands remember her to-night! Almira Fales was preëminently a heroine of the war. Yet already her name has gone by with her human life. It cannot be put into words what that human life was to her. How she loved to live! How absolute to her was every palpable form of beauty. How inseparable from her consciousness everything that she saw and felt and loved. How close she lived to Nature. How she clung to this green earth. Yet her door is shut, her gate is closed. The trees and flowers which she planted bloom on without her. That life so intense, so real, so near, now by my utmost effort I cannot touch it, nor feel it, nor realize it, although it still exists. That woman so human, so living, so loving, that it seemed as if she must live in our humanity forever, is as remote to me this moment as the most distant saint in the centuries, and intangible as the furthest seraph in the heavens. What else can so change our existence into the impalpable substance of a dream as to have such a life with us, of us, full of human love and hope and suffering, and then to exhale into the unsubstantial memory of a life gone by. The reflection of such a life might fall on one in any place. Yet here it reminds me that in no other city in the land do we walk so perpetually in the shadow of persons and of events gone by as in the city of Washington.

I sit down in the Red Room, and, looking back to the time when Mrs. Adams dried the executive linen and cotton above its bare floors, what processions have trooped within its crimson hangings. Memory leaves no room to evoke the courtly Mrs. Madison, the stately Mrs. Polk, the statuesque Miss Lane, the statesmen and beauties of generations and of administrations before the war. To remember the people who gathered here between Lincoln's first and last reception is to recall more ghosts of things gone by than one memory can conveniently entertain. Lincoln's last reception! Who that was there will ever forget it, when statesmen, generals, soldiers, common men, tearful women, and little children passed beneath the blazeless chandeliers, which had burned above so many smiling crowds, to look for the last time on the murdered Chief, whose melancholy eyes for the first time refused their gentle, human smile.

But in Washington it is rarely the dead who remind us of things gone by — it is the living. The belle of a past administration comes back expecting, without a doubt, to renew old conquests and to achieve new triumphs. The little girls whom she left in short frocks she finds in the places which she filled. She wonders what ails the faces of her friends — she left them smooth and young, she finds them lined and old — and it does not occur to her that they are making the same comments on her own. The man whom she refused in her imperious youth, because he was poor and positionless, she finds rich and powerful, with a fair wife by his side, whom she cordially hates. The old door-keepers at the Capitol, who used to swing back the doors of the Diplomatic Gallery so obsequiously at the very sight of Hon. ——'s daughter, are now among things gone by. The new ones, in the plain, middle-aged woman, recognize no former belle. They challenge her — ask her if she belongs to "a member's family." The "open sesame" has gone from her hands. She has no choice but to go to a side gallery, or to go home — which, at present, means the hotel. She still assumes "full dress," lifts a bare and bony neck above a girlish corsage of tulle, hangs the roses of June in her faded hair. But in vain. She is a queen without a throne. Her kingdom and her subjects are among the things gone by. To the careless young generation about her she is "only an old maid, who was a belle once, mamma says." She leaves the Capitol in disappointment and disgust; and she was a wise woman who said that she would "never come back again." The woman of letters, who achieved an ephemeral fame a generation past, returns to early haunts with the old ambition for adulation and power burning unabated in heart and brain. The public men who courted and flattered her, the society dames who followed her for the favors of her pen, are now among the things gone by. Instead of being alone in her special sphere, attracting public attention and admiration to herself as a solitary and exceptional genius, she finds dozens of women who think, write, and help shape public opinion, each claiming her special work, her special audience, meeting the demands of a later era of a younger generation. *She* is no longer the lone particular star, at which everybody turns to gaze both in public and private assemblies. She walks lonely and unheeded where she once moved the central object of universal admiration. If she falls to lamenting the giants forever departed; if she sees nothing but pigmies in their places; if she declares that there are no longer any great men, nor any beautiful women; that the new writers are all "weak," and writing "in horrible taste," it is very natural, but no less unfortunate; for every word she utters only assures us that she has had her day, and belongs already to things gone by. If a man who has held a high office of public power comes back to his lost kingdom (though, if he is a wise man, he never will), he finds the multitude, that once bowed down to him, all worshipping the newly-arisen sun. Is it possible? One year ago he ruled the land! Perhaps millions of money and millions of lives hung upon his word. All office-hunters, all favor-seekers, waited his call with obsequious fear. All fashiondom rolled in its carriage to his mansion in the West End. It is empty enough now. He is solitary enough at present; he has time to eat, and a good deal to spare. No impatient crowd now waiting all day for the privilege to say "Just a word." No cringing sycophant, lifting his hat in air to "Mr. Secretary," meets him at every turn. They have no use for him any longer. He has nothing more for them; and they show that they know it by leaving him behind and chasing his successor. He already belongs to the things gone by. The successful politician, whose ambition may have leaped to the highest gifts in the keeping of the people, learns suddenly some day that the great tidal wave of fortune, which has borne him so high without reaching the highest mark, is already setting backward. It has seemed so long such an easy thing to hold the balance of popularity, to be a manager, a leader, that no political triumph has seemed impossible, no prize beyond his reach. It drops like a thunderbolt some day, the knowledge that a new leader has arisen, that new combinations have been formed; envy, jealousy, rivalry, political hatred, — all are at work to defeat the man who hitherto has outstripped all competitors. He is no longer sure of his friends. Men smile in his face, and stab his reputation in the dark. They assert that he has attained the utmost reward due his powers or his service, and shall receive no more. Nor will he. He has reached his utmost mark. The wave of political favor, rolling backward, rises no more. Thus political aspirants, at the very floodtide of ambition, find that success has already rolled back among the things gone by.

A wife, in some moment of loneliness, comes unawares to the consciousness that the love which she dreamed of in her impassioned girlhood is already a thing gone by. She learns this as she slowly accepts the fact that will not be denied that the husband in whom her being begins and ends can live without her. She learns this as she waits the long hours through for one who does not come. As she waits for him, she recalls the hours long gone, when, with all the ardor of a young man's first love, he swore to her that she was all the world to him! She believed him — tender, credulous woman! And he, in his first glamour, believed himself. How bitter is her awakening! How changed is all the earth when she at last admits the fact that his life has many objects; that it is but a portion of his nature which she holds; that, if she should drop from it forever, it would flourish on no less — that he could live without her. He loves her still. When he finds it convenient to come, if he did not find her waiting for him in the accustomed place, he would look at the vacant little chair with a sense of injury. Perhaps he gives her all the time left from crowding ambitions and hurrying cares. Why should she ask for more? Is she not his wife? According to her nature, she submits to time's irremediable law. Perhaps with reproaches and tears, unfortunate woman; perhaps in uncomplaining silence. In either case, she mourns for something gone never to return — the freshness of love's first consciousness, the rapture of its dawning delight. It is love still; but it is love touched by the inevitable chill and change of experience and of time.

The mother clings to her child, and feels that she holds something in her arms that will need her forever; but the little girl grows away from her love and cherishing to the nearer love and care of another, and the little boy leaves her behind. The man out in the great world may live a life which his mother cannot fathom and never share. He may treat her with reverent care or condescending affection; he may snub and forget her; but to the mother her child is forever her child. She lives in the joy of his babyhood, long gone by; and thus it happens that a noseless doll and a battered little boot, that the baby played with or wore, cherished in some secret drawer, is dearer to the woman's heart than all the possessions which the man has won in the world. Some of the loneliest people whom I have ever known have borne and nurtured children, only to be left in their old age alone. They found all their joy in living over the years gone by; and every date resolved itself into the time "when —— was a baby."

No fact of human existence impresses me so profoundly as the individual loneliness of human life. Amid the happiest relationships, amid the most congenial of companionships, it is no less significant. The dearest cannot follow us into the depths of loss and of sorrow into which we must sometimes go down. And this through no lack of love, through no weakness of sympathy, but from human inability. They cling to us, they call to us, yet we die alone. And many more than we dream of, and they often the tenderest and sweetest of souls, in the ultimate sense, live alone. How often the dearest experiences of our human lot are partial, transitory, and unsufficing. Every joy bears one consummate flower which is never repeated. Happiness, like beauty, grows to its supreme moment; then, however imperceptibly, wanes. It is beauty, it is happiness still; but some change has touched it since its perfect hour. The flower out with nature has its growth, its perfection, its decline. No less does the human flower, in body, in brain, in spirit, follow its seasons. How beautiful, how brief they are. With the keenest consciousness of the present comes the keener consciousness of its passage. Stay, beautiful youth! Stay, thou entrancing noon! Stay, innocent love, supreme delight! Stay, calm thought, thou angel of peace! While we utter the cry, while we stretch out eager hands to detain, the boon is already among the things gone by. No entreaty can bring it back. Rachel weeping for her children did not fill the world with a deeper lamentation than the often unuttered cry of the human heart calling for the joy that was, but is not. Thus life is a perpetual mausoleum. Every day the heart buries its dead. Every day some cherished plan, some silent hope, some dear desire, goes down to its grave. We leave it behind. We go on, making no outward sign of the inward loss. But somewhere, sometime we sit down by the way, and silently count over our losses. Then we acknowledge that the treasure most deeply missed and mourned is one of which the world has no knowledge, and of which our words have made no record. The past is always picturesque. Time softens all asperities. It mellows all crudeness. The passing discord, the painful peculiarity, the personal repulsion which often jars and hurts us in the intercourse of the present lies dim and almost lost in the perspective of the past. Through its hallowing radiance the beloved individual comes back to us glorified from all defect. Life's supreme moments of blended bliss and pain lose their pangs in time ; and in memory we live them over and over again in ever new delight. Thus it is that our dead are ever angelic. Thus it is that the joy gone by is forever ideal and divine.

I have not been stringing pathetic sentiments together for the sake of being pathetic ; but have illustrated imperfectly the inexorable law of human mutation, which we must all obey. And this is the question evolved, How shall we meet and bear its penalties? With unrest? with repining? with futile rebellion? or with serene philosophy and cheerful religion? You are beautiful to-day; many worship you. You will wake some morning to find your beauty gone, your worshippers kneeling at other shrines. You have power to-day — so much it seems to you that the world, *your world* at least, could not get on without you. Some day you will come suddenly to the knowledge that your power has gone, your burdens have dropped upon other shoulders, your honors are worn by other men; and the world, even your world, gets on without you.

Life offers no lesson to mortals so hard to learn, no lesson hiding in its truth so keen a sting to self-love as this, that your prime has passed, and that you must make room for others; that the flower of your beauty, the flower of your genius are in their decline; that you must wait in the shadow, while the younger bask in the splendor that you have left behind. How few are ever willing to admit that *their time* has come to learn it. Thus it is that we see so many women refusing to grow old gracefully. Instead of wearing their years as a crown, mellow and beautiful in the light of their declining sun, they deck gray hairs and wrinkles with a hideous counterfeit of youth. This is why we see writers writing on reputations which they have long outlived; writing after they have ceased to have anything to say, except to repeat what they said better years and years ago. This is why we see men once in power still imagining themselves important, and in garrulous and impotent speech evoking the ghosts of a dead reputation in the councils of younger men.

And yet repose is not death. Rest has its recompense as well as labor. Through every mutation of our life we are followed by the divine compensations. The noon has not passed, but it soon will. In the afternoon let me renew my life in the morning lives of younger souls around me. Let me not begrudge them the youth once so bounteously bestowed upon me. They will rob no one, they will but be glad in their own share of the inheritance of being. Then let me thank God that he gave me *my* day — it's morning, its noon, its peaceful twilight shadow. Let me be glad that I *had* my day, and thus with rejoicing take my place among the things gone by.

XIV.

THE FALLEN MAN.

We see pictures of the fallen woman at every turn. In the pulpit, on the platform, we hear her portrayed with an accuracy and an unction which makes our pulses stand still with pain and horror. Why does nobody paint the fallen man? Why does no priestly voice call upon us to weep over his downfall and his shame? I see him everywhere. He came into a shop in Broadway, yesterday. His clothes were torn, his feet were bare, his eyes were glaring with the insanity of drunkenness. A wild animal could scarcely have been more dangerous. What a creature to go home to wife and children! He was only a fallen man of the most degraded type. There is a fallen man who never staggers in ragged clothes with bare feet. He stands at the corners of streets; he lounges in the doors of hotels; he emerges from drinking and gambling saloons; he comes out of the house whose door leads to death. His fall is graven on his face — in its haggard lines, in his sunken eyes, in his weary yet mocking look, from which purity and peace and the possibility of innocent happiness have gone. There is a fallen man whose garb is faultless, whose face fails to tell his story. He is never seen on forbidden ground, never in questionable places. The latch-string of gracious homes always hangs out for him. Mothers are eager to commit to his care their innocent daughters. Women beautiful and idle seek him, and flatter him on to a deeper fall. His fall is graven only on his soul; yet he is no less a fallen man. No less fallen, because only he and his God knows that the wreck of a life, the everlasting sorrow of a lovely soul lie at his door. In the gay world few reproofs are uttered, no tears are shed, for the fallen man. While he wears fine clothes, while he carries a full purse, society ignores even the possibility of his fall. His victim is shut out in shame; but the woman who makes a victim of *him* is a wearer of the purple of this world, a bearer of the pomp and triumph of life. Through so many ages man has been the acknowledged seducer of woman, the fact has been overlooked and forgiven that woman is often the seducer of man. I know such a woman — a woman of fashion, allied to a man high in position. She is a woman of large personal and mental magnetism. For what good purpose does she use it? She uses it to "attract" men from their allegiance to duty, honor, and a pure love! She boasted in a drawing-room that "she never saw a married man whose love she could not win away from his wife, *if she chose.*" "My dear husband," said a fond little woman, "you could not; nobody could take him from me." "The little simpleton!" declared the Lamia, afterward. "In less than six months she came to me crying, begging me to give her husband back to her; that he neglected her, that he upbraided her constantly because she was not more like *me.* I don't want your husband, I said; I only wanted to show you that I could do what I pleased, and to teach you not to trust in *any* man's love." There is many a Lamia. She stands the central figure of many a social circle. In silken attire, in a luxurious home, surrounded by all the alluring accessories of wealth and cultivation, herself fascinating, if not beautiful, what wonder that she draws within her charmed sphere the many homeless, wifeless, dissatisfied men of her acquaintance! The power of a woman thus poised and surrounded cannot be estimated. How does she use it? To inspire the man who basks in its splendor to say, "Such a home will I create for the woman I love, such a paradise for my children"? To encourage, to help him in the pursuit of the usefulness, the influence within the reach of his honorable endeavor? To make him in love with the strong, brave, pure manhood possible to him? No. She uses it solely to make him "fall in love" with *herself*. All the magnetism of her beauty, all the subtlety of her brain, is used to satisfy the greed of her vanity, the depravity of her passion for personal conquest. Does she know the issues in her life at stake? No matter. His wife, his children, the woman who would die for him? No matter. His honor, his integrity, his self-respect? No matter. All together are not an atom in the balance, weighed against her insatiate vanity. He, all that he cherishes, may go to rack; but she must not be denied her triumph. Some hour, when she takes off her gauds, she must be able to say, "I conquered him." She must be able to whisper in secret to the weak creature who is her "bosom friend," "I conquered him. He went down before me. I was astonished! I couldn't help it, dear! How *can* I help it, if so many men *will* fall in love with me?" Does the Lamia ever incur any danger? No. The Lamia can *always* take care of herself. She plies her victim with beguiling flatteries; she bewilders him, between childish smiles and tender tears — never shedding enough of the latter to make her nose red; she astonishes him with her subtle wisdom; she is artlessness, she is innocence, she is angelhood personified; she is Psyche and Circe combined. Then, after having roused every slumbering impulse and passion of the man, if, in an unguarded moment, he betrays his weakness, *then* she is majesty astounded and virtue on a pedestal! Then, when no longer his own master, her bright doors open and shut on him. He goes forth into the night, out into the darkness. To what? To whom?

Who will say that woman is in no way responsible for the fallen man? The woman who walks the streets in open shame we may follow with pitying lamentation. The woman who, through the weakness of her will, through the magnanimity of her affection, which can never be measured or fathomed, stakes all her fate in one frail human heart, gives more than her life to one erring man, is one over whom the angels in heaven must weep in compassion.

But she who, wearing the garments of affluence and of influence, still uses the gifts and graces of her womanhood only as decoys to lead men astray; who, in the guise of innocence, would steal their birthright of honor, blur their perception of purity, demoralize their affections, madden their passions; and then, having proved her power over them for all evil, sends them forth into the world to betray and to rob the weak and unfortunate — she is the woman who is a disgrace to human nature. God may pardon her; but the woman who respects herself, who loves woman, who honors man, never can. Is it strange that the average estimate of women by men of the world is so low? that, herding together, they speak of women in language which even they would blush that their mothers should hear; that each man, shutting from his memory the pure angel of his earliest youth, sneers at virtue as a fiction, at the purity of woman as a fable and a dream?

No one but his mother, his sister, or his wife weeps for the fallen man.

This is one of the saddest mistakes of our world; one for which all humanity suffers — viz., that purity, demanded imperatively of woman, is deemed impossible to man. Where is the safeguard to society? Where its exalted standard? While men are left to believe, and to act accordingly, that virtue, in the sense in which it is expected of women, is not within their power. The practical working of this theory makes each sex but the prey to the other. This will always be, till the standard of virtue in woman is made also the standard of virtue in man. It was a great and pure man who uttered these words: "The world will never be better till men subject themselves to the same laws which they impose upon women." It was a man said this. Were it a woman, all the apostles of license would at once declare that she said it, because, being a woman, she could not know what man is. I do not forget what human nature is, in its universal and unchanging essence. I do not forget in its best estate how frail it is, how easily overcome; nor forget the inevitable modifications of life and character resulting from the varying laws of temperament, of sex, of physical and mental organization. But neither the history of polygamy or of monogamy, Campbell's "Philosophy of Marriage," or Leckey's "History of European Morals," or the history of the whole life of man in every race, and through every age from the beginning of the world till now, can make me believe that man created in the image of God, man immortal as his Sire, man the head of all human intelligence, through all his earthly life, is at best but little more than a bundle of blind instincts and of lawless appetites, at whose mercy he is, which he is as powerless to control as the beast at his feet. This brutal idea is the underlying impulse of polygamy, of all the lasciviousness, license, and barbarism on the earth. The sister is taught, whatever her temptation may be, that she must be good; the brother is left to believe that, however he tries, he cannot help being bad. It is expected of him that he will grow to be a respectable man some day; but before that event, through the law of his nature, he must necessarily be very wicked. The sister is taught that she must preserve herself blameless for the future husband to whose life she is to be the crown; the brother is left to spend the same time "sowing his wild oats." To his wife he is to bring no virginity of heart, no purity of person, no record of a stainless past! Many a man looks into the eyes of the wife, who trusts him as she does her God; into the faces of his daughters, who believe him to be scarcely lower than the angels, with a secret remorse which cannot be measured, as memory forces in upon his thought what he has been, perhaps what he is. With what shame he is conscious that, if they knew his secret history, he would stand transformed before their eyes; that, to remain what he is in their thoughts, he must hide forever from their knowledge the crimes of his youth. Young man, remember this! The dearest reward that can come to you in this world, is a real home — the love and faith and help of wife and children. Remember this, while striving with foes without and foes within. If you *will*, you *can* live worthy of your heritage. You can cherish a faith in human goodness; you can cultivate personal friendship with noble men and women; you can fill your life with honorable occupation and cheerful recreation; you can "steep your soul in one pure love;" and, trusting in God, you will never be a fallen man. The grandest object this side the throne of God is a perfect man — a man powerful in brain, powerful in frame, with conscience and will ruling over the animal force which makes the puissant basis of his manhood. The saddest sight on earth, is such a man in ruin. By the height of what he might have been do we measure and deplore the fall which makes him what he is. Passion may be grand; but it is passion in obedience. Appetite is not ignoble till it debases the soul and triumphs over purity. With our finest theories we cannot make this crooked world straight. But each one may make it so much the better and brighter by at least the character of one individual. When shall we have purity in our lives? When peace in our hearts? When joy in our homes? It will be when woman feels a deeper responsibility for her personal power over every man who comes within her influence; when that power is tested and controlled by a healthy conscience and a pure heart; it will be when she ceases to regard every man that she meets as the legitimate prey to her vanity, as a tyrant to be turned into a slave, as a Sampson to be shorn of his strength. It will be when, with true recognition and reverence, she meets the royalty of manhood with the royalty of womanhood, saying: "If thou art the world's king, I am the world's queen!" It will be when man tests all his relations with woman by the same code of impartial honor which makes him honorable among men. It will be when he who scorns to be false to his comrade, will scorn equally to be false to a woman; when he shall cease to stoop to subterfuge, to deceit, to falsehood, to keep peace with numbers of women, to each of whom he is personally committed, over all of whom he desires to exercise a secret, illegitimate power. It will be when each man seeks in each woman something of that divine quality of womanhood which even the basest man desires to find in his mother, in his sister, in his wife. It will be when each shall cease to say: "I will absorb, rule over, possess this creature of God." It will be when both shall seek in the other their noblest friend, their truest and dearest companion; when the woman shall revere the man as man because he is worthy of such honor, and the man revere the woman as woman because she commands his reverence before she wins his love. Then we shall not have the cause that we now have to weep over the fallen woman and to bow our heads in shame before the fallen man.

XV.

PHYSICAL BASIS OF STATESMANSHIP.

A PORTRAIT of Mr. Gladstone in a number of "Every Saturday" is very suggestive of Mr. Fessenden. Indeed, it seems almost as if it were Senator Fessenden, rounded out into ampler life. It is what he would have been if his body had equaled his brain. Of the two, the English premier's head is less powerful in development than that of the American senator. There is less height, less width, less causative fullness in the frontal dome. But any slight discrepancy here is more than atoned for by the capacious nostrils that give air to the brain-cells, the great throat, the broad shoulders, the grand enginery below which propels this brain and sustains it. What might not Mr. Fessenden have been with such physical adjuncts? With them he would have been still on the earth, and in the Senate. He would have been building up a grand record for history, recording for posterity works more immortal than the "Juventus Mundi." Here the pious thing to say would be that he is "better off" — so much better off among the seraphim than in the Senate. I'm not going to say it. I prefer an honest hobby to dishonest cant; and it is very dishonest cant to be constantly attributing to the "Lord's will" that for which we ourselves are to blame. When the minister said it, "It is the Lord's will, and marvelous in our eyes," I used to cry. Now the same words in the most pathetic quaver only move me to send him "Hall's Journal of Health," or some other journal on hygiene and dietetics equally sensible. It need no longer be "marvelous in our eyes" why so many are cut off in the midst of their days. Hygienic law cannot banish death; but it can prolong existence. This law of the Lord of life and health defied and broken every day costs the nation many of its most illustrious children. We have more occasion to be concerned for the bodies of our public men than for their brains. If they took a little more intelligent care of the former, there would be less trouble with the latter; and how many splendid lives would be spared to the public service and to the hearts that love them. It is the manner of all who visited the Congresses of the last generation to come back to the new-winged Capitol, and in its garnished chambers lament the Corinthian and Doric halls of the old House and Senate, and more the eloquence vanished and immortal, of their most illustrious legislators. "If you could only have seen Calhoun and Clay and Webster! If you could have heard them!" Well, I never heard them, and never saw them. But I have giants of my own, whom I deplore no less devoutly. Seven seasons in Washington are sufficient to make one a veteran, without having seen the gods of the earlier decades. I have attained the dignity of reminiscence.

In my little nook in the gallery I murmur of changes; inquire as sadly as Elia for "the old familiar faces;" and to the neophyte beside me whisper of greatness gone, of giants departed, with all the lamenting unction of a mourner of the last generation. If, in addition, memory compelled me to mourn Webster, Clay, and Calhoun, my grief would be too much, and I should be obliged to stay at home. As it is my dear "I," I will confess to you that to my vision the Senate looks quite askew. I have tried to adjust old seats and new senators with satisfaction, and have failed. My private opinion (which, as usual, I am making public) is, that a number of these gentlemen might quite as well have stayed in their native wilds, or be still pursuing destiny, "carpet-bag" in hand. It is very evident that they do not belong here. It is not in their poor power to reflect any lustre upon one of the greatest legislative bodies of the world. This being true, *why are* they here? Shall politics, trickery, and money buy seats for third-rate men in this august assembly? They do. Mr. Muddlebrains takes his seat. He who by the birthright of God would adorn it, serve and honor his country in it, stays at home — at least, that is where he very often stays. In personal aspect the Senate has retrograded within four years. Among all its elders, one looks in vain for two such "grave and reverend seigniors," two such grand old men, as Foote and Collamer, of Vermont. Senator Cameron carries his seventy years straight and stately as a winter pine; but he has not the noble head, the open, large expression, the grandeur of mien, which made these men the most senatorial of senators. And who, looking down on his wonted seat, can cease to mourn for Fessenden, the great debater, the incorruptible statesman, the irascible, sensitive, loving-hearted man! Not in his seat, it seems as if, waiting a moment, we should see him meditatively pacing up and down behind it; or slowly slipping through the door of the cloak-room, his hands in his pockets, his slight figure bent, his great head — so much too great for the frame which could not support it — always drooping forward, as if weighed down with thought, his lips compressed, his expression one of weariness, often of pain. The longer we look the more we miss his presence, and the more unreconciled we feel to his untimely taking off. The longer we listen to a dry dribble of talk, the more we long to hear pierce the dullness one of his old keen, incisive sentences, cutting straight to the marrow of things. Without him his long-time generous antagonist, Sumner, finds no foe at once so provocative and worthy of his speech. Trumbull, more pugnacious and irate, lacks the far sight and wide mental comprehension of Fessenden. Charles Sumner still sits the grandest figure of the Senate. He sits as he sat years and years ago. Life, which leaves its subtle tracery on all our faces, has laid its hand heavily on his, as it always does on the face of a man or woman in whom existence is a battle, not a dream. The evening gray has fallen on his hair, the trace of many an inward and outward conflict is graven in the strong features; but he has still unbroken what he had in the beginning, that which is indispensable to the successful statesman and orator, — "the physical basis of oratory." Without his six feet of altitude and his thunderous "ayes and noes," Charles Sumner could never have been Charles Sumner. If he had been compelled by feeble lungs and a defective throat to shriek his dictum in a shrill treble or in a squeaking pipe, he could never as a statesman have been at once the king and the conqueror of an idea. If he had been as little as Lord Russell, not even Sydney Smith's excuse to the disappointed farmers of Devonshire, — "that he was naturally bigger, but had been reduced by his labors in the cause of reform," — could ever have given him that personal impressment which now, by filling the eyes and ears, more than fulfills the prestige of his name. Without special premeditation, I have strayed back to the thought from whence we started, — the physical basis of the statesman. For lack of it Fessenden died. For lack of it, and it only, he missed the highest intellectual success; without its ministry even *his* fine brain could not fulfill its loftiest function. For lack of it some of the most intellectual men in the Senate to-day are slowly dying. This would be altogether too gloomy to talk about if it were too late for remedy. But it lies within human power to stay the prodigal waste of human life which marks us as a people. Think of the havoc which death has made among the most intellectual and illustrious of our race within two little years! Even while I write, the land is mourning for one the bravest and best beloved of its soldiers, who lived through a hundred battles, to fall dead in his prime. Looking at the magnificent physique of General Thomas, who can believe that by the laws of Nature and God he should have perished in the perfect flower of his years? Thus too many Americans perish. The English statesman, with his athletic habits and out-of-door life, carries on his physical and intellectual power unbroken beyond the years of threescore and ten. Past that age we often find him bearing the heaviest responsibilities and fulfilling the most active duties of the public service.

Thus, with scarcely any relaxation of intellectual vigor, Lord Palmerston served his country to his eighty-second year. Lord Lyndhurst made two of the most powerful speeches of his life at the age of eighty-six, and died at the age of ninety-three. He was an English American. If an American statesman was not dead long before that time, the man who wanted his place would declare that he ought to be. The rare American who lives to such an age is usually spoken of as a second child, who has long outlived his time. While the average American statesman, no matter how superb the stock of vitality with which he begins his career, usually manages to consume it so prodigally and irrationally that, with bad air, bad hours, and bad habits, exhaustive labors, and inadequate relaxation and exercise, inordinate ambitions, contests, and excitements, finds himself an aged man in middle life; a victim to incurable disease, or the ready prey to imminent and hopeless paralysis. This is not a very animating picture of American physical deterioration, and the most painful feature of it is that it is true. One thing I shall never be able to understand: that is, how a being arrogating to himself such immense superiority as man, — one who in normal strength of nerve and muscle and will often is so superior, — should yet quite as often, through his entire human existence, violate and outrage the laws of his physical life, and in controlling impulse and appetite show little more than the resisting power of an idiot or the strength of a child. If you are tempted to think this an exaggerated statement, just recount the names of distinguished men who actually murdered themselves by over-eating and drinking. How many thousands more have done this whose names have never been written.

Excepting, perhaps, a dozen really noble-looking men, the United States Senate has nothing to be proud of in its external aspect. The remainder are a mussy and inferior looking company. We have a right to be disappointed in them. In the House of Representatives we expect to see a heterogeneous assembly, typical of many climates and conditions. But from the Roman to the American Senate the inflexible idea of a senator has been that of an eclectic, eloquent, wise, and august man. If a man possessing no one of these qualities still by some circumstance obtains a senator's seat, I know of no patent that he holds to high esteem because he has filched a name which he does not honor.

XVI.

INSTINCTIVE PHILOSOPHERS AND STATESMEN

THE one-eyed philosopher of the "Edict" sees acutely on one side; but he is as blind as a bat on the other. His text is "Mind's the standard of the man;" and he goes on to show that he believes in brain and not in body, and to prove that the instinctive philosophers believe wholly in body and not at all in brain. According to his one eye, the "Instinctives" are a set of lunatics, who in this world of absolute facts are yet content to lift their faces to the sky, and swear incoherently by the representative words of Truth, Justice, Mercy, and Purity; men who put words for ideas, instincts for intellect, inspiration for reason; despisers of brain, whose chief strength lies in the use of capital letters and exclamation points. Having made these assertions, the one-eyed philosopher of the "Edict" thinks that he has done the clever thing, and feels much relieved. Is it not a partial and one-sided thought which discusses the mind of man independently of bodily conditions? Is not a man's brain more dependent upon his stomach than his stomach is upon his brain? We are no more all intellect than we are all instinct. There is no fact more significant than the dual life of the human being. The "Edict" may publish another loose dissertation on this material thought; but it cannot destroy its truth, that "man is man only by virtue of his blood." If every thought involves the death of an atom of the brain, its exquisite loss can only be supplied by the vivid current from the heart which feeds and vitalizes it. If this be diseased and depraved, the organ of thought is touched with its disease and its depravity, and the very thought evolved is more or less tainted and morbid. If "mind" — or, rather, character, the finest emanation of the intellect and heart — "makes the standard of the man," how puerile to discuss that standard while ignoring the contributive conditions which fix irrevocably the quality of that mind and character. Perhaps it is very clever in the "Edict" to cry out: "Is there some one of the organs in his square-built, well-put-together body which gives him absolute truths by process of secretion? Has he glands that would give us a good bill to regulate the civil service of the United States?" But all this cleverness does not annihilate the fact that more than one "absolute truth," and many "bills" in Congress have been defeated and destroyed through the "processes" of diseased "secretions" and through "glands" which refused to perform their functions. It is because we believe in the supremacy of reason and of the moral faculties that we insist that the highest health and perfectibility of the human body is necessary to their perfect development; and insist upon it as a general axiom no less because we remember several geniuses and a few saints who managed to exist in bodies which were daily insults to their souls. In this life, at least, the spirit of man cannot act independently of the material organs through whose medium alone it finds human expression. Robust vitality may exist with a coarse brain and an obtuse organism; and a large brain of fine fibre for a season may struggle and assert its inherited power though impeded in its action by vitiated blood. In defiance of morbid conditions, it is able for a time to assert the laws of its primal inheritance. I am thinking of two of our own statesmen, born giants in intellectual strength, who now in middle life are bowed down with more than the infirmities of age. A powerful intellect in a powerful body was God's birthright to each. If they have cherished the first, they have outraged the last. They have destroyed the perfect mechanism through which only their intellects can act; they have broken Nature's sacred laws till they are objects of pity, in their mental and physical pain — till there is nothing left for them but suffering, and the certain grave a few months further on. The spasmodic action of their powerful minds is like the fitful flare of a dying flame. In the sudden and transient gleam we are painfully reminded of what the steadfast light of such intellects might have been, sustained by strong and steady health. We can illy spare them from the legislation of the nation. They should have grown old in age and honors in its counsels. Not the "weighty matter of government," nor judicial study, nor devotion to "reason," has made this impossible to them; but the transgression of physical law has brought physical death as its swift, inevitable consequence. Even the reasoning faculty, which our one-eyed philosopher does not too much exalt, cannot long exist unimpaired in the defrauded and degraded body which he despises. And, though he were to sneer on through every column of the "Edict," it would not annul the truth that temperance and cheerful health must form the basis of mental and moral greatness. And though he, gratuitously, utterly condemns and rejects our definition of a great man, his condemnation is not frightful. If we have a great man, he is great from no intellectual power *solely*. That he could be wholly great without intellectual power, or if he were not a master of knowledge, or of thought, no one would declare. But all experience asserts that the intellectual power must wear the crowning more. Beyond the command of knowledge, or of thought, a man must be master of himself to be wholly great; if not, his imperfect greatness is a mockery and a shame. That superlative purity of the moral nature may exist with no commensurate intellectual stamina we are all aware; a man may be great in goodness only, and through lack of mental power totally unfit for the administration of public affairs. But what the public service needs, what it demands beyond the force of language to declare, is the absolute man: a man in whom the moral forces are as perfectly developed, as keenly conscious, as the quickest of his intellectual faculties; a man who, whether he looks up, or down, or straight forward, can declare that he loves truth and justice, mercy and purity, and prove by his own character and in every public and private act that he does so love. The one-eyed philosopher laughs, and sets these words in the mouth of a school-boy, to prove that they cannot make *him* great; but he takes nothing from their significance when they are meant and when they are lived. Why this outcry for despised "goodness," for incorruptible men in high places? Because it is the deepest need of the state. If the need were for intellect, the demand would be for that; the demand is for intellect exalted by conscience. The government has never suffered for lack of intellect in its administrators; but it has suffered and does suffer for their lack of conscience. We take it for granted that the men who are sent to Washington to administer affairs have brains; we wish that we could take it for granted that they have integrity also. The truth is, there is a kind of "smartness" coupled with unscrupulousness which has learned the trick of buying place and patronage, and eagerly pays the price for both, which just now is uppermost. If the secrets of the government in its various departments could be published to the people, they would find that what they need most in their public servants is not mere intellect; but a finer honor, a stainless rectitude. They want men whose votes and influence can neither be bought nor sold. Is it womanish and old-fashioned to demand such men? Not while the government remains with the people. Have we a Utopian ideal of excellence for men in public life? Not at all. But this is true: only men of positive moral strength are equal to its exigences and its temptations. Mr. Congressman came to Washington an honest man. In his quiet country home he had never been tested beyond his strength; had never grown entirely away from a simple and natural life. Once here, the evil forces of an over-stimulated life begin to play with desire, and conscience, and will. Undreamed of ambitions, a lust for gold and for power, take possession of him. Besides, Mrs. Congressman wants a coach as fine as Mrs. Senator's; her establishment must be as expensive, herself and her children as lavishly arrayed. That all this can be done with the congressional salary is impossible. Now comes the test. Here is a thousand dollars for a vote, and thousands more to secure a man a place high in government patronage; the "Whisky Ring," the "Treasury Ring," and untold speculations. If he sells himself to these interests through the weakness of his will, this man, supposed to be legislating for the people, becomes simply a political gambler, like any other gambler, living by his wits and the tricks of fraud and chance. We have no romantic notion of asking congressmen to emulate gods and angels, or of demanding their freedom from human infirmity, or of asking them to lift their faces to the sky to swear at random their fealty to any lofty principle ; but the people whom they represent have the right to demand that they should have the moral strength to refuse a bribe, and, striving with evil forces within and without, yet be strong enough to be true to that which is best in themselves.

The "Edict" portrays the "Instinctive Philosophers and Statesmen" as "scorners of reason" and of common sense, expending their fervor in "double-leaded invocations to Eternal Justice," and in a frantic use of words to which they apply neither meaning nor practice. That the most profound words in human language are often used idly and for mere effect no one will deny. Thus used and abused, they yet lose nothing of their distinctive significance. *They* mean no less. If "words are the only things that will last forever," it is because they represent that in man which is eternal. They are the visible signs of his finest emotions, of his subtlest thoughts, of his rarest aspirations ;

or they are the embodied types of the degradation and the slavery of his soul. To *be* that which the highest words in human speech represent is the consummation of human character. And to know what you mean, and to mean what you say, requires more than a one-eyed or an instinctive philosophy.

XVII.

PIN-MONEY.

"LADY SOPHIA is to have £16,000 jointure and £400 pin-money," said Horace Walpole of Lady Sophia Fermor, when she became the wife of Lord Carteret, — a lady for whom (although a younger son) Horace had dared to cherish more than a passing fancy. While English law has never hesitated to appropriate the whole of the wife's fortune for her lord's benefit, English custom has always taken care to provide her bountifully with pin-money. In this respect the Englishwoman is more independent and happy than her American sister. As a rule, the English wife has the absolute control of a certain sum appropriated to household expenses and her own personal wants to a much greater degree than the American woman. In this respect, at least, she is freer, happier, and more self-respecting. The very responsibility tends to cultivate in her sound judgment, forethought, foresight, and prudence in expenditure. A creature treated as a child in the use of money will seldom have more than the judgment of a child, albeit it be that of a child of larger growth.

The very extravagance of a large class of American women springs from this mode of treatment. Impulsive as children in their desires, they exhibit no more than the judgment of children in their expenditures; hence the enormous "bills" which confront the husband and father, filling him with wrath or despair, in which state he is so often portrayed tearing his hair or taking with violent hands his own life. That men suffer much from the thoughtless extravagance of women is beyond question. It is a fruitful source not only of unhappiness, but of vice. Young men, deterred from marriage by horrible forebodings of milliner, dressmaking, and furniture bills, enter into social relations which blight their lives and in innumerable instances make a happy family life for them impossible. If the girls of wealthy families were educated to a wise knowledge of the uses and possibilities of money, to the responsibilities which its possession involves, to habits of thoughtful expenditure, with a definite income settled upon them, within whose limit they were to bring the gratification of their personal wants, what a decrease there would be in the habit of careless, useless shopping; in exorbitant bills; in a blind, reckless extravagance, which neither knows nor counts the cost of anything on which the fancy may happen to light! Our family monetary system in this country is all wrong — in ten thousand instances ignorantly, carelessly, not willfully wrong; no less its hard penalty is paid by ten thousand unhappy hearts, in society and at home. If its result is extravagance and questionable modes of making money, — is recklessness and suicide among the more wealthy and fashionable; in average American life its sequence is niggardliness, misunderstanding, discontent, estrangement, and unhappiness. Money in some phase is one of the most fruitful sources of unhappy family life, especially of unhappiness between husband and wife. This is true, while American women as wives are among the most indulged women on earth. This is one trouble; they are simply *indulged*, in greater or less degree; and mere indulgence necessarily infers dependence on one side and supremacy on the other. It is the fitful emotional kindness of a master; not the just sharing of an equal. This, carried into the minute money-need of daily life between two persons (so often mentally on a par) living in the relation of husband and wife, is the source of immeasurable discord and sorrow. In this relation impulse may be good when it happens to be generous and tender; but justice is better. Just here is one of the most painful illustrations of caste in sex, as developed in daily life. I know men — good, kind, manly; who would risk their lives to save their wives in danger, who love them, after their own fashion — to whom it never occurs that their beloved are not among the happiest and most blessed of women; who would declare me insane if I were to say that they did their wives injustice and made them unhappy every hour in the day. Yet I do say it, and say it because I love the wives better than the husbands; although the latter, as men go, are very admirable indeed.

There is Dove-eyes. She was one of the ten thousand girls of whom North America has such just occasion to be proud, — sensitive, refined, intelligent, well-educated, self-supporting, high-spirited, honorable, tender, loving, and lovable. Dove-eyes was the daughter of necessity, and for years had supported herself and helped others by the honorable toil of her hands and brain, when she succumbed to her especial fate in the shape of Alexis, to her the Grand Duke of all men — indeed, a god walking the earth. Out of her woman's small pay she had saved a comfortable *dot*. When, as his wife, she entered her Grand Duke's palace, which was small and on an unfashionable street, she carried into it from her own small earnings furniture to furnish it, a handsome wardrobe, and a small bank-account book of her own. But when she married Alexis she gave up all her opportunity of independent support. Henceforth she was to work, and to work hard; but she was to work only for Alexis. He was her sole employer. Did he pay her as justly as strangers had done? We shall see. While painting pictures, after the manner of men in love, his favorite one had been of the lovely time coming when she would no longer have to toil for a living; when it would be his joy not only to provide for every want, but to anticipate it before she knew it herself; and when her chief business would be to put on her loveliest dress and freshest ribbons, and wait for him with a smoking dinner ready, which (in the picture) involved neither care nor labor to cook. Nor did Alexis shirk the actual demand upon himself necessary to the carrying out of his desire. He was what in larder parlance is called "a bountiful provider." He made handsome presents at intervals to his wife, and he said: "My dear, if you want money, all you have to do is to call on me." It sounded beautifully. What could be more generous? Both were very much in love, and for a time all was blessed. Alas! the most ample trousseau will wear out. Pretty wedding frocks will grow old-fashioned and take on a look of antiquity. Babies are little cherubs who need many clothes, which they outgrow with a frightfully rapid impunity. I am sorry for everybody who has not a baby, yet no one will deny that it is the most costly of all God's gifts. What suffering, what anxiety, what money it costs to convey it safely from the first tooth to the last one of all dreadful baby diseases! Dove-eyes woke up one day, to find that her last pretty dress had been cut up for baby; that the last cent of her own little bank-stock had been paid out for baby — for extra doctor visits, extra diet, extra airings, for many nameless little needs, which a man would never dream of, but which are no less necessary for that. Alexis would think them unnecessary. Dove-eyes believed them to be indispensable — life itself to her and baby! She woke up to the still more bitter consciousness that she had not a cent of money that she could call her own; not a cent that she could spend as her own necessity or judgment dictated. This, hard to any woman, is especially so to a woman who had always had her own independent resources, however small; who had always had her own small private fund, on which to draw for her own personal necessities. Hard as it was at first, she had tried to overcome her reluctance to ask Alexis for money. "It was foolish and over sensitive not to be willing to do so," she said. It was wrong in her to feel as if it made her seem like a poor dependent to come and ask her husband for what she needed. Did she not at home work as hard and for more hours than he in his counting-room? Indeed, her work now was never done. It used to be she could sit in the evening and read. Now baby cried so she could not even listen to Alexis read the evening paper, but had to carry baby off out of his father's sight, that his cries might not prevent his comprehending the evening news. Had not Alexis said that "all he had was hers?" She had tried to think of this, and to ask for a few dollars just as if they *were* hers, which he held in trust for her benefit. Alas! after the first or second trying, it was a miserable failure. She had asked when Alexis happened to be cross or short of money, and he exclaimed: "Why, what have you done with the last? Gone already?" She ventured to say that it had gone to the doctor; when Alexis responded: "I must say, Dove-eyes, I think your fears for that child make you send for the doctor oftener than is necessary." Dove-eyes was not sure that she didn't. She tried to put down her own sensitiveness, and still go to Alexis for money when necessary. But so often there were notes (oh! how she dreaded those dreadful notes; they seemed to be forever due); or he was "hard pushed;" or, at last, he exclaimed: "Dove-eyes, I must say that I think you spend some money unnecessarily, and not with the best judgment in the world." As he went over the little account of personal expenditures, he found: "Charity, 50 cents." "Just now, charity, with us, must begin and end at home," he exclaimed. This was too much for Dove-eyes. The first time that he had ever rebuked her with real harshness. She poured floods of tears upon baby's head, in the little cupboard aloft where she rocked him, until even baby grew loving and dumb under the piteous shower-bath. Dove-eyes never asks Alexis for money now for any personal want whatever; though, in an abundant home, the want of it is a perpetual thorn in her heart. Amid plenty, she has not a penny that she can call her own, to expend as she pleases without rendering an account to her husband. Poor Alexis! He meant all that he said in the happy honeymoon days about "anticipating her every want." He intended to do so then. He intends to do so still. Only, what man ever lived who, by virtue of his masculinity, *could* anticipate every need of a woman? As a bachelor, without an atom of personal experience in that direction, he thought it would be delightful to anticipate and provide for every want of his lovely wife. How much the most economical of woman's needs might cost he had not the remotest idea.

Alas! Dove-eyes' needs, in a very great degree, only represent the wants of the household, the never-ending, ceaseless demand of the family. To supply these always, smilingly, spontaneously, ungrudgingly, under the stress of difficulty, of business losses and business worry, was not so easy. What wonder that, amid all, the personal needs of the woman were at last lost and overlooked altogether. Yet never for a moment has Alexis meant to be other than generous to his wife. The failure lies not in his intention, but in his fashion of carrying it out. If in the beginning he had said: "Dove-eyes, we are not rich: but, with care and thrift and God's blessing, we may become so. My average income is so much; let us divide it. Here is so much per year toward the payment of our home, so much for table, with a margin for hospitality. Another (however small) for charity and for the rainy day. So much for personal expenses, yours and mine. Here is your pin-money, Dove-eyes. It is yours absolutely. I shall never ask how you have spent it, or if you have spent it at all; but I shall pay you your share just as regularly and promptly as I would any other equal partner. As we are prosperous, it shall be increased to the limit of my ability. Our home is deeded to you. Whatever may happen to me, you and the children will not be homeless." What a proud and happy Dove-eyes she would have been! What an impulse, what an incentive would have been given her to cultivate prudence, wisdom, and economy in this proof that her husband trusted her, and acknowledged her his equal partner in the life-long home company.

As it is, Alexis wonders, with all his efforts to make her happy, that Dove-eyes should so often look worn and unhappy. Sickness, the care of her children, the natural wear and tear of human life, cannot account for *all* the sadness looking forth from her soft eyes. Dove-eyes is very much in love with Alexis still. There are a hundred traits in his character to make and keep her in this all-suffering state. She never misses an opportunity to tell her friends that he is the "best man in the world." She believes it, though she often makes the assertion with a little inward sigh, which nothing outside of her own heart hears. Yet, with all her love and his, there is a shadow on their wedded lives, which justice, just a little justice, added to the love, could lift and disperse forever.

Alexis would think it most outrageous if Dove-eyes were to call him to an account for every penny he chooses to spend for cigars, for newspapers (whose unnecessary and unmanageable accumulation is a household nuisance), for his soda-water, his "treats" to his friends, in which she has no share; his hundred unaccountable ways of spending money, in which masculinity delights and for which it never renders account.

If Dove-eyes called him to account (which she never did), how he would resent it! "Isn't it *my* money? Don't I earn it? I shall spend it as I please!" That is just what the man in him would say; and in these words all his man's injustice to the woman whom he loves would come in — "my money," not "our money." Dove-eyes works. She works hard, without wages. She does not earn *money*. "I *give* it to her," says this munificent Alexis. "I mean to be a liberal as well as loving husband, and *give* her all of my money that she needs. How much she needs, and for what she needs it I am to be the judge. To be sure, she cannot judge for me — how much I am to use as a person, or for what purpose I am to use it. It is not her right. I am man and master, and earn it; and shall say just how every cent of it shall be spent."

In all that she has suffered and borne for him, in the constant care and toil of years, the wisdom, the self-denial, the economy with which she has saved and garnered what he provided — has she earned less than he?

Even if this were possible, in giving herself, her life, her love, her devotion for all time to him, did she not relinquish forever the opportunity to earn or to accumulate for herself personally in any other profession? Does he owe her nothing for that? In choosing the highest of any profession on earth to woman — that of the wife and mother, as her husband's partner in every home interest — should he treat her with fitful indulgence, even in little things, or with the tender honor due to an equal? Dove-eyes feels that their home is "her husband's house." She doesn't feel at liberty to spend one shilling out of the common fund for any charity or any purpose dear to herself, because she *must* tell Alexis, and she is almost sure that he would find fault, or hint at her lack of judgment, till she would be altogether miserable; and sure, judging by treatment received, that she was personally little more than a mendicant in her husband's home of plenty.

There are many Dove-eyes. There are many Grand Dukes, whose name is not Alexis. Yet men marvel at the unrest of American women, and discourse with great eloquence and ignorance on the subject.

Let me astonish you anew, gentlemen, by assuring you that the lack of pin-money is at the bottom of much of it. Dove-eyes will never do any such thing; but thousands of women do. They start off in the most unthought of tangents. "Anything, anything," they say, "that brain or fingers can devise, whereby I may earn a little money that will be my very own, that I can do as I please with, unchallenged, or without any man telling me that he *gave* it to me, and that I must do just as he says with it or do without it."

Not a man in the world, no matter how just, how generous he is, can know how much his wife (and the more sensitive and delicate she is the more so) must sometimes suffer through the very fact of financial dependence. You may be truly the best husband in the world; as a rule, she may be glad that all her temporal blessings flow to her through you; and yet there will be times when she will suffer through this condition most keenly — when she would gladly part with her dearest treasure to possess a little money utterly her own, which she might use for some purpose dear to her heart, without asking any mortal for it as a gift. My dear brethren of mankind, do you not see how much misery you can make and can unmake in your own homes? After all, his use of money seems to be the utmost test of a man's manhood? Touch his money-nerve, and you measure him in almost every other direction. Yet remember, it is not so much the amount of money you share, it is your way of sharing it, which makes her happy or unhappy.

When you are tempted to patronize your wife, to make her feel in any ignoble way her dependence on you, if you could but remember one thing — that the true woman who gives herself for life to be the wife of the best of men, to love him, to suffer for him, to bear from him all that a woman must, to toil and suffer for his children, places him under a debt of gratitude which no money on earth can repay! Considerate care, love, honor, and justice can be the only recompense. To be sure, you are a Grand Duke. Nobody denies that; you have only to prove the patent to your rank. Leave your wife to be Grand Duchess, and in her own realm (which, surely, is not yours) let her reign with equal freedom and in equal justice sovereign over her own pin-money. Justice in the household coequal with love will do more than ten thousand treatises to quell the public outcry and soothe into peace the just discontent of women.

XVIII.

BREADMAKING.

"MAN cannot live by bread alone," it has been written; yet it is very certain that he cannot live without it, and is but a poor creature if it is not of good quality. This is what ails half the men we meet. The women who pretend to take care of them, and complain so much because they have to do it, feed them on such wretched bread, to say nothing of their other edibles, that no wonder they are thin, yellow, haggard, jerkey, and don't believe in "woman's rights." It is perfectly natural, if a man sees that the woman he knows best has reached no high standard of excellence in the arts peculiarly her own, that he should doubt the capacity of all women to fill the higher callings which even now open but a contested sphere to their ambition and effort. My good sisters, if you wish to convert these masculine creatures to your most progressive ideas, you must begin by feeding them on good bread, which beginning will probably involve the necessity of knowing yourself how to make it and bake it. Make it with your own hands; sponge it, mould it, bake it, this poetic bread — fine celled, white, tender, and sweet. Stir it, beat it, and bake it, this still more delicious bread — brown, fragrant, life-feeding, full of fibre for bone, full of phosphorus for brain. With this perfect bread build up the muscular, nutritive, and nerve systems of this perturbed mortal, who does not believe in your "rights"; and when you have thoroughly "re-constructed" him on a sanitary basis, he will declare to you of his own accord: "Do anything, be anything you can. I make no objections, providing you continue to feed me on ambrosial bread. It is fit for the gods." But, my poor brethren of mankind, when I meditate on the concoctions of saleratus, grease, and vicious acids of all sorts which are given you to replenish the lost atoms of your material bodies, though it may not be in my power to admire you, I could both pity and pardon any mental or moral obliquity of which you might be guilty. The human blood cannot be fed with poisons, or even with indigestible food, and yet the brain and heart maintain strong and healthy action. In knocking about the world, how long we live and how far we go to eat one piece of superlative bread. Among the Arabs poor bread is a cause in law for divorce.

Breadmaking in its perfection has become almost one of the lost arts.

Is there any other people who take such infinite pains to be fine, and so little to be comfortable! One cause for this is that all household service for women has fallen into disrepute. The science of domestic economy, than which none requires finer qualities of brain and heart, is now entirely ignored, under the contemptuous epithet of "drudgery," from which the chief object of a woman's life must be to escape. One of the most mischievous qualities of this ignorance is that it is usually very proud of itself. I know the matron of a public institution, who thinks it very vulgar and unladylike to think or to know anything about your food before you sit down to it. One result of her sensibility is, that the amount of hot saleratus-cakes, sour and leathery bread, greasy and dried-up meats demolished in this institution are appalling to contemplate. Appalling because of the numbers of teachers, young, half-fed girls, and orphaned little children who sicken and die for lack of nourishing bread and seasonable fruits, while there is enough worse than wasted in food that cannot be eaten to procure both. This institution is supervised by wealthy and intelligent women, who supply everything for its inmates but properly cooked food. Probably it never occurred to them to ask the matron if she ever visits the kitchen. She does a great deal of praying; which is excellent so far as it goes, but never went so far yet as to take the place of practice.

I believe religiously in the thorough physical and intellectual education of girls. But that girl is not educated, who, having mastered every other science, is totally ignorant of the chemical properties of a perfect loaf of bread; and who cannot, upon necessity, make such a loaf with her own hands. The gauge of education is not what we have studied; it is that which our learning has made us. The only measure of discipline is its result. "What am I? what can I do? what can I be for my own help and the help of others?" is the first question which every young woman, on leaving school, should ask. The most that the average girl who leaves the average boarding-school can answer is, that she is "finished." She *is* finished. Her digestive organs are finished, her nerve system is finished, her poor little muscles are finished, her feeble brain is nearly finished. She is an overwrought, hysterical, dyspeptic creature. She subsists on pickles and preserves, hot cakes, strong coffee and tea, and over-spiced meats. She has no domestic nor physical education. She violates, without knowing it, the laws of human health every hour of her life. Without one atom of the development necessary to fulfill the true duties of a womanly life, she is told, perhaps, by her "pa" that her "sphere is home," and that she must stay there. No noble ambition, no useful employment, no sweet home duties fill her days. She spends most of her time crimping her hair, eating candy, writing gushing letters, and dressing for the coming man; or she sits from morning till night in a cushioned chair embroidering slippers and smoking-caps for this possible husband; or she may study a French cook book long enough to learn how to make a fancy cake or concoction whereby to woo him through an epicurean stomach, with an accompanying, "I made it." But where is the maid whose matrimonial line — whose pretty covert, "Please marry me, sir," — is ever baited with a good honest loaf of bread, kneaded and baked by her own hands? Instead of deeming it a degradation or a misfortune that she does not know enough to take care of her health under ordinary circumstances, it is the supreme delight of her existence to be "in the hands of her physician," and to enjoy the perpetual felicities of being "delicate." "I am *so* delicate," said a girl to me, in the same tone in which she would have said, "I am so happy." "My daughter is *so* delicate," we hear mothers exclaim. From watering-place to water-cure, they go about with their languishing burdens. It is "my daughter," "my daughter," everywhere, always; her weakness her delicacy, her innumerable ailments. It never occurs to these anxious women that this very daughter is a living protest against their own ignorance and inadequacy to fulfill the first duty of motherhood. And here I make no allusion to inherited or constitutional disorders, to which all may be innocently liable; but the functional ill-health caused solely by false habits, false food, and ignorance of the laws of physical life. The trouble is, it is fashionable to be delicate. A certain undefined reproach is attached to robust health. To be really elegant, really intellectual, according to the accepted standard you must look "delicate." There are men as well as women who believe that a certain appearance of sickliness is indicative of high intellectuality; as if a torpid liver could ever supply blood and brain as well as an active one. What is worse, the odor of sanctity has attached itself to wretched health. At one time dyspepsia was a synonym for piety, because nearly all clergymen had it. And eternity alone will reveal the numbers of feeble and frightful sermons which have been born of the pickles and preserves fermenting together in the dyspeptic stomachs of good men. And it will take the same limitless length of duration to inform the women of the world how much they have done toward making clergymen an enervated and sickly race of men, by the indigestible mass of goodies with which the individual woman of all generations has persisted in piling the plate of her "beloved pastor." All the early saints were "ashamed of their bodies;" and if many modern ones are not, they ought to be. It was centuries before Christ that the heathen Plotinus first declared himself ashamed of his. After such cycles of time and of knowledge have passed, it is a mournful fact that so many Christians ought to be ashamed of theirs for the same cause. The only pride which the Latin Fathers took in theirs was in declaring what wretched tabernacles they were of parchment skin, and bones that would scarcely hold together. Ever since their day, saints and sinners, each according to their fashion, have done their best to punish and degrade the body — the fair and marvelous human home which God deems fit for an immortal spirit. Yet the first hope of the race lies in the purity and perfection of the body. A brain of remarkable organization may accomplish vast results for a time, in defiance of vitiated blood and disordered functions. But the most powerful brain, the most exquisite nerve-life, cannot long exist unaided by an adequate muscular and nutritive system. A mind perfectly powerful and harmonious cannot inhabit a diseased and morbid body. If, as a nation of dyspeptics, whose brains flourish at the raw expense of their vital forces, Americans have accomplished so much, what would be the ratio of their performance if their mental and physical development were commensurate? This brings us back to our breadmaking — to bread as the deepest root from which must grow the perfect flower of body and brain. Never was a nation fed on more wretchedly-made bread than ours. This is man's wrong; woman inflicts it. A man may build a bigger ship than a woman ever can; but he never can make better bread than she can, if she only will. Do you ask me if I believe in woman drudgery? Never. Extreme poverty involves a degree of drudgery which can never be escaped.

God knows that there are poor, overworked women whom no earthly power can help, unless He lift from their weary shoulders their too heavy burdens. I am not talking to them;

but to the woman who, with ordinary health and adequate means of support, yet regards all household care as so much " drudgery," which, in proportion to her " sense of superiority," she must escape. If you are a drudge, it is not because you are mistress of a house or a family; but because, being both, you lack the education, the discipline, the devotion which only can make you adequate to the highest duty and dearest delight which can devolve on woman. You are a drudge because you are too ignorant, too indolent, or too indifferent to impart to your servant the simplest lessons of intelligent domestic service. Your house is disorderly, your food wretched. You fret, you complain, you cry. Your husband scolds, perhaps swears. You are all sickly. Your doctor bills are enormous. Your sole consolation consists in exchanging miseries with your female friends. Suppose you possess the practical knowledge to teach your servant how to prepare every dish necessary to a perfectly supplied table; suppose you often made with your own hands its white and brown and golden bread; suppose you devoted the time which you now spend in crying and complaining in studying practical hygiene and chemistry in their relations to cooking (even then you would not be frightfully wise); suppose you gave the time now consumed in nursing your sick children to studying the laws which govern their little bodies, in learning the properties of the food necessary to their nourishment; suppose you spent one quarter of the money which now goes to the doctor, in securing them healthful amusements, and the time which you now devote to worrying your husband to mutual recreation and companionship; would you be more or less of a drudge than you are now? There is something false and wicked in the cry which denounces the domestic duties of women *as such*, which must finally react upon and destroy itself. Let us exalt our homes, if we would exalt ourselves, our children, or the man whom we love. If we have a home, let us deny the idea and prove it false in our own personality that it is *necessary* to go higher than that home, to neglect its duties, to ignore its privileges, in order to secure the most harmonious development, the widest culture, the profoundest influence.

The increase and perfection of machinery have taken the distaff and the needle from the hands of women. The decrease of marriages, the changes in scientific and intellectual opinion, are among the causes which every day are opening and widening the employments and opportunities of that large and constantly increasing class of women who are entirely dependent upon their own efforts and attainments, not only for their subsistence, but for their place as human beings in the world. What just mind will say that all legal disabilities should not be removed from their way? that every employment and profession should not be opened to them, to fill according to their culture and capacity? The world-wide change now going on in the condition of women is but the natural result of the primal law of growth and fruition. Womanhood has not yet grown to its perfect prime, has not yet borne its most consummate flower. Growth and fruition do not involve chaos or destruction; but law and order, harmony and love. Then how querulous and weak the outcry of fear for an impossible future. No change can outpass its natural limit. No change can wash away the ineffaceable life-marks, rooted in human experience, the indestructible affections of the human heart, eternal in their life, as the law and order of God.

When woman ceases to be imprisoned by necessity in a house falsely called a home; when she is no longer compelled to live in it a slave for the mere chance of material subsistence; then she will gladly turn from the outer turmoil of the world to a true home as her best refuge and surest chance for happiness. Then she will realize, as she never realized before, that to make that home all that it should be, all that it may be, demands not only the graces of the heart, but the highest intellectual gifts which a human being can cultivate.

To-day, that woman who brings the ripened powers of a rich and disciplined intellect to the ordering of every department of her household; who makes her home the centre of light, beauty, and intelligence, drawing the weary and the homeless into its radiance; she who every morning sends forth into the world a brave and happy man; who every day gathers into her rejoicing arms joyous and beautiful children; she who from the exceeding riches of her life and love gives, yet is not impoverished; who, doing, being this, is a free woman, — free in body, free in brain, free in spirit, free in the largest right of her humanity, — she is the crowned, the triumphant, the blessed woman.

XIX.

OUR KITCHENS.

"COÖPERATIVE kitchens!" Heaven forbid! Heaven probably will not interfere; but surely women will. If there never was a house large enough for two families, there never will be a kitchen large enough for a dozen. It is not strange that some women want to get rid of their kitchens, such looking and smelling dens as they are, and will always remain. Cowper sung "The Sofa," and glorified the teacup. I proclaim the kitchen, with a hearty desire to rescue it from its abused condition. It is nonsense for men to bemoan their grandmothers, because they spun and wove, while we do neither. If they worked perpetually, you may be sure that it was because they had to, not because they wanted to do so. They would have been just as glad to have availed themselves of steam-looms and sewing-machines as a refuge from endless drudgery as their granddaughters, if they had only had them. Yet it would be vastly better for our generation if we consulted those dear old ladies oftener than we do; better if we imitated them more closely, not in their piety only, which on the whole was of too self-abnegating a sort, for it did injustice to some of the best powers which God had given them and increased the depravity of man in making a bigger tyrant of him than even nature intended. But there is no danger of our imitating them too nearly in their personal interest in their kitchens. It is for the woman of the nineteenth century to hold in her development the equal balance of physical and mental culture. She cannot do this and neglect her kitchen. No matter how far at times she may rise above it, it will always do her good to come back to it; and, if it is the kitchen that it ought to be, she will ever feel delight in returning to its homely brightness and savory smells. I am sorry for that woman who does not treasure in her heart somewhere the memory of a beloved kitchen. Perhaps it was grandmother's kitchen, or mother's. May be it was in the country. You can hardly be happier in heaven than when you played on its floor a little child. I love such a kitchen; not the discarded one of a fine villa, but the honored kitchen of a thrifty farm-house. It faces the east, and takes the sun's first "good-morning." Thus its busiest hours are full of brightness, and its restful afternoons full of serene light and peaceful shadows. Its wide door opens on a grassy yard, where "the old oaken bucket hangs in the well." What a yard it is! Its clovery grass is a paradise for bleaching; its irregular paths run through the dandelions down to the garden whose luscious vegetables offer a daily market for the ready hand, and out to the orchard where the ruddy apples hang. There is an old lilac bush by one window, a sweet-brier by the other, while morning-glory bells cluster about both. Beside one is a stand full of plants, which in the winter flourish in the morning sun. On its ledge there is a work basket — a marvelous basket — into whose depths I sometimes dive, through piles of stockings, through bundles and bags, through scissors and thimbles and pins, down to a needle-book (certain to be at the bottom, if only through my impetuous poking), in whose pocket I am sure to find a whole literature of domestic recipes, heart-poems, and editorials on the state of the nation. Beside it is a little old chair with a warm cushion. This is the mother's chair and this the mother's corner, and not to be invaded. Then the old kitchen has a deep fireplace, a vast bake-oven, and a modern stove.

It has a great pantry, whose wide shelves are filled with glittering milk-pans, all set for cream; and a store-room, in which you may find everything for cheer, from the barrels of flour and sugar, the rows of sweetmeats, dear to every housewife's heart, to bunches of dried catnip hung up for the cat, and pennyroyal enough for every stomach-aching baby in town. The old kitchen floor is painted a clear gray, brightened by gay home-made mats. It has a deep-throated clock, that rules its days; a book-rack filled with books and newspapers, and colored prints on its walls. It has an arm-chair, a sewing-chair, and a chintz-covered lounge. There is nothing in it too fine for its place. It is only a kitchen, after all, yet a joy to behold and to enjoy.

There is a parlor in this house, proud in a bright grandmother-made carpet, of the most intense stripes; in haircloth furniture, as shining as a beetle's back; in a profuse pile of old daguerreotypes and a new photograph book. On its walls old gentlemen sit in venerable frames, with high collars, stiff enough to break their necks; and old ladies sit in others, in mutton-leg sleeves and bristling caps, who look down with mild severity on the chignons of their descendants. When the minister comes, or the children from town, this parlor is opened and furbished. But, somehow, sooner or later all the company gravitate back into the old kitchen; for the glow, the cheer, the love are there.

Then I am in love with a kitchen in town. If it is not as poetic as the country kitchen, it is more convenient. My heart has thrilled with delight at the sight of its bright yellow floor, and exulted with conscious thrift while I turned the faucets of its "stationary tubs," and tested the virtues of its "spacious range." Who can portray the splendor of its pantry — its mugs and jugs; its "nests" of polished boxes, whose covers shut in the priceless berries and spices of the East; its rows of glass jars, filled with glowing jellies — the ruby of the raspberry, the purple of the blackberry, the crimson of the currant; its shelves of canned fruits? There are peaches for you; tomatoes for *you;* sweet corn in this can that will give you succotash in January, and delude you with the make-believe of an August feast. This kitchen's window lets in the sunshine; and its back-door opens on a grassy plot, on which the clothes may bleach, the dog may play, or the baby roll. And all around the stone walks runs a border of flowers: and, if morning-glories don't hang on the window, they do on the fence. There are but few city back-doors which do not open on a yard as large as this. Show to me one pure with grass, fragrant with blossoms; or show me one nauseous with the *debris* and refuse of the house, and I will tell you the sort of people who abide inside. You tell me that my kitchen is not practical? That I don't personally know about it? I know *all* about it; which is more than I can say of anything else. I know that every kitchen must have its soapy days, its sudsy days, its codfishy days, and even its cabbagy days — that, in spite of its posies and spices, its odors must sometimes be more pungent than pleasant; but I know also that we may open the windows, let the bad air out and the blessed air in, and that through and beyond everything remains the kitchen, all that it should be, or nothing that it should be, just as we have made it! Everybody knows the charm of a pleasant parlor. Every woman likes to display her taste and refinement in it, according to her means or culture. All its pretty nicknacks have a price for her heart which no money could pay. Its statuettes and pictures, its soft sofas and chairs, give us the refreshment of beauty and the proffer of rest when the day's work is done. The parlor is the crown of the home ; but the kitchen is its heart. In the parlor may bloom the flower of its culture ; but the root of its comfort is in the kitchen. The parlor may reveal to us the exact standard of a woman's taste ; but the unerring interpretation of her disposition is the kitchen. Wealth or circumstance may place the actual labor and duty of your daily life outside of your kitchen. Trained servants may make it unnecessary that you should fulfill its daily tasks with your own hands. But has it ever occurred to you that, however exempt yourself, *some woman's life* is lived in your kitchen, and how much you may add to that life by making your kitchen a pleasant place to inhabit ? She is no less a woman in all her native susceptibilities and needs because she is poor and does your work. Do you realize how much every life takes on of the hue of its surroundings ? And what a minister of good as well as a minister of beauty you may be when you make your kitchen perfect *as a kitchen*, as you have already made your parlor as a parlor ? It cánnot be measured, the wretched health, the morbidness, the misery, the vice even, which have had their birth in the dark, unventilated dens which are called kitchens, in which so many women drag on their weary lives. And when the girl of our time grows up to regard the kitchen of her home as something more than a hole to be shunned, in which Bridget was born to drudge; when she brings into it, instead, her calico apron and smiling face; when she devotes to its service a portion of the cultivated powers now wasted in idleness, if not in sin, we shall see the beginning of that royal race of women for whom we longingly wait, and in whose advent we so devoutly believe.

XX.

CASTE IN SEX.

I.

IN KNOWLEDGE.

After the disastrous result of Eve's first nibble at the apple of the tree of knowledge, and the awful penalty which it entailed upon her daughters, it is not wonderful that for many centuries they were too frightened to follow her example. Nor should we fail in charity to the sons of Adam (no one of whom is over fond of work) to say that together they have done their best to shut away the forbidden fruit of wisdom from their sisters, in bitter remembrance of that first taste which cost Adam his spiritual supremacy and fore-doomed every son of his to the curse of labor. At any rate, ever since that unlucky beginning man has done his best to keep woman in ignorance; and, after having met with a very tolerable success in so doing, with a charming and characteristic inconsistency, he now declares that her lack of acquired knowledge is the sign and seal of her mental inferiority to himself. In this arrogant declaration he does not take cognizance of the fact that through all the earlier ages of human existence it was physical force which held in abeyance the brain and soul of the human race. The creature the physically weaker was the subject creature. In its abject condition intellect, spirituality, aspiration went for naught. Out of man's primal brutality, out of his instinctive, unrestrained appetite, muscle, and will, every form of human servitude, every shade of human ignorance has grown.

"At the beginning the earth was without form and void, and darkness was upon the face of the deep. The SPIRIT OF GOD moved upon the face of the waters. *God said, Let there be light, and there was light.*"

The physical chaos of creation was not deeper or more dreadful than the mental and moral chaos which succeeded the Fall of Man. We are just emerging from it. We have not yet escaped it. But to-day, as at the beginning, it is Spirit brooding over Matter — illuminating, inspiring, triumphing over it — which brings light into this troubled world. Two forces have always pervaded the universe: the unseen and the seen, the material and the spiritual. Man represents the material, woman the spiritual — the masculine and the feminine. These forces are but just beginning to reign together in equilibrium. Man has been woman's master because he has been the physically stronger. Woman is ceasing to be man's slave, because, in the equal development of the human race, brain and soul in her are coming to prevail over the merely selfish and material in him. To-day the manliest man would be ashamed to look into the eyes of the woman by his side and tell her that he is the master, because he could knock her down with perfect ease, and break her bones with much greater facility than she could his. And yet, out of man's brute nature, out of that most ignoble in himself, has come his loudest assumption of superiority, his longest and lowest tyranny. Every day the human race is moving further and further away from the supremacy of brute power. Yet long ages to come must pass before woman can outgrow, mentally or morally, the marks of her manacles. The man born and bred a slave, even if freed, never loses wholly the feeling or manner of a slave. The woman born to physical subjection and degradation can never seek or use knowledge as her birthright. Never till she holds her sex in honor, as man holds his, can she be his equal, even in her own realm. The deepest insult which can be shown to a human being is to associate it solely with material functions, with no cognizance and no consideration of its intellectual and spiritual power. This insult, through all ages, man has offered to woman. That it has come from man proves his inferiority to her in the very element of her nature which he ignores and insults. She has ever delighted to honor him in his loftiest attributes. She pays homage to his intellect, his soul. She worships in him something beyond sex, which will live glorious forever. While she, reaching out through every impulse of her heart, to the sweetest in human affection, through every faculty of her brain, to the highest in nature and art—she to him has been chiefly the creature of his pleasure. Being this, whenever and howsoever she has proved herself to be more, by so much he has deemed himself defrauded, and proclaimed loudly that she had outleaped her sphere. Man, mighty in brute power, and by that enthralled to his senses, through it has made woman his subject and slave. That he might make her these more utterly, he began by declaring that she had no soul. She was naught but a body, and that body was his. Struggling, aspiring under such a ban, do you marvel that woman through soul and brain has wrought little? Marvel more that she has wrought anything. China boasts of the most ancient civilization of earth. Its system of scholarship is the most minute, intense, and exhaustive in the world. Yet, within a year an imperial mandate has gone forth that no Christian teacher can open within its walls a school for women; that every one already established shall be closed. Is it strange that the Chinese woman believes that, if true to certain vows while living, after death she will return to earth in the form of a man? To her, with his immunities, that seems reward enough for all she suffers or loses here. Athens, the home of beauty, the focus of learning, of art, of æsthetic amusement, of political freedom, worshipping the form of woman on every shrine, made her a prisoner in every home. Every Greek pulse thrilled with life and action; every Greek heart throbbed strong with the passion of freedom; every Greek eye craved the divine harmony of beauty; yet the Athenian woman, within sight of all, yearning for all, embodying all, was shut into a sordid, slavish existence, or seized freedom and culture at the price of infamy. An Athenian, in open court, telling how good a husband he was, began in this wise: "As a husband I rendered her situation agreeable, but as a woman she was left neither the mistress of her fortune nor of her own actions."

Nearly three hundred years ago a young girl in Dijon, France, conceived the insane and profane idea that even girls should learn the alphabet. She appealed to her father, who was a member of the Provincial Parliament; and he consulted four doctors of law, who decided that it was "a demoniacal work for *girls*" either to teach or to learn the alphabet. Whereupon the sons of Dijon arose in riot, and stoned Françoise de Saintonges for her wicked designs upon the understandings of her sisters. She, nothing daunted, took fifty livres, all she had, hired a little house, and with five other maidens entered it. It took all her money to pay her rent. "We have no beds," she said; "but we spend our nights in prayer." The craven father relented sufficiently to send from his abundant table cold victuals for herself and maidens. They went on from the alphabet to learn many other things. Twelve years from that day on which they were stoned Dijon held high carnival in their honor. Forth from their humble house walked a hundred maidens, clothed in white, while the bells of the city rang and the people strewed flowers in their pathway. They were preceded by the entire Provincial Parliament, and by all the soldiers of the province, to the stately building which stands to-day in Dijon, a monument to the everlasting glory of Françoise de Saintonges.

The first thing that the Pilgrims did, after planting themselves in Boston, was to found a school for boys. Their sisters cried so loud for the forbidden fruit of knowledge that the city elders were induced to open a high school. Immediately its doors were thronged. With ninety-nine boys two hundred eighty-six girls appeared as candidates. Worse — after the alphabet and figures, they aspired to Latin and Euclid. The city council met, and resolved that this immoderate zeal for knowledge was too much for the man-nature to bear. In eighteen months the school was finally closed, because of its multitude of scholars of the proscribed sex.

Yet no less a woman was the first instigator of Harvard College. Lucy Downing, imbued with the caste of sex into which she was born, was one of the ten thousand women who sacrificed themselves and their daughters for their sons. She was the sister of Governor Winthrop, of Massachusetts, and sent her daughters into service, and lived poorly and meanly herself, that "her George" might be educated. In October, 1636, she wrote from London to her brother, the Governor: "If God should call me, I could go far *nimbler* to New England if a college could be established there, which, in my opinion, would put no small life into the plantation, besides being of incalculable benefit to George. The result of this sisterly appeal was that in 1636 the General Court of Boston voted four hundred pounds to a college, to be established in Cambridge. In 1640, second on the list of the first graduating class was George Downing, the nephew of Governor Winthrop. George Downing lived to serve with distinction under Cromwell; to be a "turn-coat" under the Stuarts; a baronet, and "a great man," who snubbed his mother and refused her money when, at the age of seventy-three, she asked him for it. It was then that she wrote to one of the sisters whom she had put out to service for the sake of this brother: "Your brother George has bought another *town*, but more your brother George will not hear of for me. He says that it is only covetousness that makes me ask for more." Yet in his unfilial thanklessness George Downing did not differ in spirit from thousands of learned professors and popular ministers of the present day, who, having been educated at the cost of devout women, who had left their own daughters untaught to educate other people's sons, now shut in the faces of women the doors of the very colleges which could never have existed without them.

II.

IN EDUCATION.

After the fate of the first Boston high school open to girls, it can hardly be accepted as proof that the Boston woman was intellectually the inferior of the Boston man, because as late as the day of John Adams, while Harvard College lavished all its opportunity of education upon him, she was denied the privilege almost of learning how to spell. Barely to read and write decently, with the knowledge of dancing, at that time made up the sum total of a woman's education. Yet, in defiance of it, out of her clear, strong head and deep, loving heart, Abigail Adams wrote letters to her son, John Quincy Adams, which, with her example, made the strongest moral force in his education, and which will live in literature as long as any speech of her more liberally educated husband. It proves how much more powerfully is one human being individually than any statute of law which proscribes it or oppresses it; that in all ages and conditions women have existed who, through sheer mental and spiritual force, have commanded wisdom and the reverence of men in the very face of the sneer, "You are *only* a woman." We need not go outside of our own race or language to learn in defiance of what ridicule and prejudice they did it. A few sentences from Swift's famous letter "To a Young Lady on her Marriage" will indicate to what stage the education of women had advanced in the age of Queen Anne. He says:—

"It is a little hard that not one gentleman's daughter in a thousand should be brought to read or understand her own natural tongue, or to judge of the easiest books that are written in it; as any one may find who can have the patience to hear them, when they are disposed to mangle a play or novel, where the least word out of the common road is sure to disconcert them. And it is no wonder, when they are not so much as taught to spell in their childhood, nor can ever attain to it in their whole lives.

"I advise you, therefore, to read aloud more or less every day to your husband, if he will permit you, or to any other friend (but not a female one) who is able to set you right; and as for spelling, you may compass it in time, by making collections from the books you read.

"I know very well that those who are commonly called learned women have lost *all* manner of credit by their impertinent talkativeness; but there is an easy remedy for this, if you once consider that, after all the pains you may be at, you never can arrive in point of learning to the *perfection* of a *school-boy*.

"Your sex employ more thought and application to be fools than to be wise or useful. When I reflect on this, I cannot conceive you to be human creatures, but a certain sort of species hardly a degree above a monkey, who has more diverting tricks than any of you, is an animal less mischievous and expensive, might in time be a tolerable critic in velvet and brocade, and, for aught I know, would equally become them."

History has not recorded how refined or sensitive by nature the English maiden was who received this letter from Dean Swift; but any woman of sensibility in the present day can easily decide how much such a letter would encourage herself in the pursuit of learning. Only sixty years ago Sidney Smith wrote that there was no rational defense for the great disparity between the education of men and women in England. The advance is great; yet to-day the spirit of Caste in Sex prevails in the education of women both in England and in America. Never till the human race outgrows it can simple justice be meted to woman in any life or work that she attempts. Never till she commands her faculties and functions as man commands his can she be judged justly in love, in learning, in labor, in creative art. Never till she has outgrown and outlived the caste of sex in herself can she command the high justice which all women long for and a few so loudly demand. She has yet to realize — or, at least, to act as if she realized — that, whatever ideal of excellence a woman commands, she must command it as woman, not as man. Ever since the world was made, women have been abused for being women, till the brightest of them have come to despise their own sex, to apologize for it, to abuse it, or to try to be above it. For centuries a woman believed the highest compliment a man could pay her was to tell her that she was "superior to her sex." If she was ambitious and wanted to do something great, she tried to do it *like* a man; and, of course, made a miserable failure. To-day the most "advanced" women think it necessary to talk and act like men, as if there were any special honor in *that!* A witty woman, anxious to impress a man with her wit, in nine cases out of ten falls to ridiculing her own sex, its weaknesses and foibles. The man may laugh, he may even admire her brilliancy, but by so much must she sink in his esteem, if he holds her to his own code of honor. If not too self-absorbed, she would notice that he offers her no antithesis in himself by ridiculing his own sex. A man is proud of being a man. He has pride of sex; he holds his own in honor. In nine cases out of ten a man is true to all other men. He will hide rather than expose the faults of men; if he cannot justify them, at least, he covers them with silence.

A woman, if not ashamed or sorry that she is a woman, is so imbued with the conviction that her sex is held in latent contempt that she deprecates or apologizes for it, if only to prove to the man with whom she converses that she is superior or indifferent to it, that by so much she personally may rise in his estimation. A race that does not believe in itself can never rise above the level of slavery. A sex false to its own highest possibility, a sex not true to itself, must accept degradation. A woman would despise a man who habitually ridiculed or sneered at men, at whatever work they did or attempted, however poorly done; she would despise him as a man false to his own sex, to his own manhood. Is it any less false or despicable for a woman to do the same thing? The unity of manhood makes half its grandeur.

The unkindness or indifference of woman to woman makes half the weakness of womanhood. When women are as true to women as men are to men — when they hold their womanhood as men hold their manhood — as a glory, not a shame — then and not till then will they rise to the dignity of a united, concentrated, distinctive force in the universe. Not till then can the masculine and feminine soul reign in harmony. Then woman will be content and proud to reign as woman; she will have no desire to rise above man, will see no special advantage in being like him. She will hold the equipoise of the human race in abiding *with* him his equal counterpart, and her glory will be the glory of WOMAN. That day is not yet. Caste of sex in education, with its root far back in the centuries, blossoms outside of all schools, and bears baleful fruit in millions of human homes. How often does a mother take her growing girl and boy and teach to each as only a mother can the mystery of the other's nature? How often does she teach each to revere the attributes of the other, teach both that in the very difference of their nature and lot they are not to fear or despise, but to cherish and love each other. Instead, as a rule, the boy is simply left to take in prejudice and presumption on the score of his sex from a thousand sources. How early the brother learns to lord it over his sister, simply because his parents allow him to do so. He robs her of her treasures; he shuts her out from pleasure with the cry, "You sha'n't. You're a girl!" He learns, from a thousand careless words uttered every day in his presence, that he is of greater account than his sister, because he is a boy; that he can enjoy many things of which she is deprived, because he is a boy; that great hopes are centered in him, solely because he is a boy, and very few in his sister, because she is a girl. She may have the quicker intelligence; but she is cut short in her studies because she is a girl. There may exist the same need that she should be taught self-help as he; yet she is left to grow in helpless, untaught dependence, because she is a girl. She may have the same longing as he after free scope for her powers; yet no less they are dwarfed and denied, because she is a girl. After such a process of education from infancy, is it strange that the brother grows up to believe that he is the superior being, not because he has given any proof of it whatever, but solely because he is a man? Or is it strange that the sister begins the life of womanhood mentally maimed, crippled through all her nature, feeble and aimless, when for not one day of her existence has she been allowed to forget that she is a girl, and solely because a girl, proscribed in every sphere of development. A man's arrogance and tyranny seldom begins by his own fireside. It begins far back, when a little boy he played with his sister. Not nature, but his mother, with caste in sex, has made him what he is, and made his sister what she is.

Not long ago a boy ten years of age burst into the room where I sat with his mother, and, throwing his books upon the table with great violence, his face flushed with passion, he exclaimed, —

"I'll *never* go inside of that schoolroom again."

"What is the matter, Ernest?" asked his mother.

"They have given me a woman for a teacher; and I won't be taught by a woman."

"Has she been unkind to you, Ernest?"

"No; but she *is a woman*. All the boys in B. will laugh at me when they find out my teacher is a woman. I never had a woman for my teacher, and I never will."

"Don't you know that some of the greatest men who have ever lived in the world were taught by women when they were much older than you are, Ernest?" I ventured to ask.

"I don't care," exclaimed this young citizen of America. "*I* ain't agoin' to be! Boo-hoo! boo-hoo!"

"There, don't cry, Ernest," said his mother. "If you feel so bad about it, you needn't go any more. To-morrow I will look you up a new school. I'm sorry, though, for Mr. ——'s is one of the best in the city."

Hearing this, Master Ernest wiped his eyes and his nose, seized his cap, and stamped forth in triumph, to tell the boy next door that *his* mother wouldn't send *him* to be taught by a woman!

The boy had passed one crisis in his life, to travel (spiritually) downward toward meanness and tyranny. Had his mother said: "Ernest, I have perfect confidence in Mr. —— and in the lady he has placed over you. You *must* go to your teacher," the boy would have learned two lessons — alas! unlearned — which would have changed his entire character: first to obey his MOTHER; second, not to despise his teacher *because* she is a woman.

Who can say that already in his heart the boy does not despise his mother; or that when, as a man, he shall despise her still more for being a woman, she will not deserve her fate?

XXI.

WOMAN SUFFRAGE.

DR. BUSHNELL admits too much in his statement of the question in the first chapter of his book to be able afterward to maintain his argument for limitation and subjection with force or even dignity. Once allow, as Dr. Bushnell does, that women should be educated with men, that the training of universities, the opportunities of the learned professions should be open to them, and after that it would be utterly useless for Dr. Bushnell or any man to mark the exact boundary of progression to a human being thus disciplined and educated. She alone could find the limit in the constitution of her own body and mind. When she had reached it she alone could know; no outside mind, though peering through the spectacles of a Doctor of Divinity, could inform her. Her capacity could be the only measure of her function. When he first became aware that men and women were being educated together in the colleges of Oberlin and Antioch, Dr. Bushnell says: "I confess with some mortification that when the thing was first done I was a little shocked even by the rumor of it. But when I drifted into Oberlin, and spent a Sunday there, I had a new chapter opened that has cost me the loss of a considerable cargo of wise opinions, all scattered never again to be gathered." All the danger and wrong now predicted as the most direful result of men and women participating in the right of suffrage, was more than foretold as the inevitable result of their being educated in the same schools. Dr. Bushnell says: "Our new codes of training are even a surprise to us; compelling us to rectify a great many foolish prejudices that we supposed to be sanctioned as inevitable wisdom by long ages of experiences." Well, Dr. Bushnell, if you live long enough, you will find yourself compelled to rectify some more very foolish and feeble prejudices which you have set down on your pages as the very essence of "inevitable wisdom." It is not likely that you are very much more "shocked" on the verge of the "Gulf of Female Suffrage" than you were twenty years ago over the prospect of women and men going to school together. You declare now that no harm, but "beneficial results," have come from that. Suppose that you wait till "woman's suffrage" is tried, before you decide whether to work yourself into a very painful state of "horror," or to bestow upon the enfranchised sex your benign and smiling approbation. No harm has ever yet befallen the world through the open, honorable association of men and women, either in education, church, or state; but unutterable harm has come through their covert and hidden relations in every age of the world and in every sphere of life. Woman in politics! Woman has always been in politics. The question is not concerning the fact, but its relations. Shall woman remain forever in government a covert, irresponsible, unacknowledged force; or shall she be trained to high, responsible power — to be honored no less as woman, wife, mother, and friend, because she represents herself in the laws which concern her, her children, her property, no less than man? How could Dr. Bushnell have proved more utterly the weakness of his own argument than by taking refuge in the proposition, that the principle of human liberty as embodied in the Declaration of Independence is the "doctrine of the woods," a "scheme of free-thinkers and 'malignants' like Rousseau and Voltaire." After informing us that he does this "for the purpose of taking down a little our egregious opinion of the suffrage," and that it will come to its end and disappear "within a comparatively short run of time," no one need wonder that he turns so lovingly to the Chinese, adding: "God forbid that *they* ever be so far captivated by our dreadfully cheap way of suffrage as to give up their cadetship way of promotion for it; a plan that has put the *whole nation* climbing upward, and will keep it climbing to the end of the world." And this from an evangelical clergyman concerning a people who, with hundreds of thousands of authors and a literature reaching back past the siege of Troy and the days of Pericles, to-day, in the nineteenth century, murders half of its female children at birth; and who, with all its competitive examinations and intense scholarship, has not a school nor a book in all the land for the *mothers* of its people! If the ideas of republican freedom are only "catch-words of liberty;" if the principles of the people's government, bought at such cost of life and treasure, are only "glittering generalities;" if we are to go back to oligarchy, or "one man power," nothing more need be said either about manhood or womanhood suffrage. But we may thank God that no wave of an ecclesiastical hand, nor stroke of florid pen, can blot out the principles of human government, dearer to the American people than life itself. It is only by denying the principles of that government that Dr. Bushnell can escape their conclusions. Once admit man's natural right to suffrage as a human being, and by no logical process can you deny it to woman.

Dr. Bushnell takes vast credit to himself, and calls on all women to note that he puts his *ipse dixit* in a much pleasanter form, with less "pounding emphasis," than the apostles. He adds: "Of course, Paul did not know everything, whether about women or on any other subject." After such a clerical admission, he cannot well call any woman "unorthodox" or "infidel," if she coincides. It is true that Dr. Bushnell on every page shows a disposition to put his lordly statements in the least disagreeable manner possible. His intention is to be *very* generous; but he is generous, patronizing, tender even, in an overshadowing, Olympic sort of fashion, that might be provoking if it were not ridiculous. Personally full of amiable feeling toward woman, he makes as many concessions to her demands as are possible with his unutterable man-conceit. The inexpressible sense of superiority which he feels *as* man to woman as woman, his delight in his own "sway-force," so pervades and prevails over him that, unconsciously, apparently, it makes him contradict his own abstract statements of the question on every page. Nothing could prove more clearly than his book that what he calls "a reform against Nature" is simply a reform — an irrepressible protest from woman against man's natural conceit, against his assumptions of superiority as man over her as woman. Of course, this is nowhere more apparent than when Dr. Bushnell speaks of woman's ministrations in the Church. What a comment is it on the bigotry of his brethren to say that *his* conclusions are far in advance of most evangelical clergymen of our day. How many of them to-day are willing to give the largest interpretation to the words of St. Paul? Who are willing to acknowledge that many of the specific reasons, customs, and laws on which those words were based have long since passed away; and that with them should have passed their restrictions also? Only God can measure the narrowness, the littleness, the personal meanness, which has ruled in the Church under cover of the words of the great Apostle! What has not woman given to the Christian Church? She has lived for it, she has died for it. The idols of her heart, the costliest treasures of her fortune, she has consecrated to it. Through all ages she has been, in the largest measure, its brain and its soul. Yet to-night in how many Christian conference-meetings and prayer-meetings could she rise to tell in simple utterance "what the Lord has done for her soul," without being challenged and silenced by some sanctified masculine warden of the tenets of St. Paul? I can count the years on my hands since I heard a New England pastor's wife, a holy woman, who rose to speak a few words of personal experience in a Sabbath-evening prayer-meeting, silenced by one of her husband's deacons.

It is amazing to see with what a majestic sweep of the pen Dr. Bushnell disposes, in three or four pages, of the great female reigns of history. There is no argument here. The greatest facts of the past are all ignored. The reign of the great Catherine of Russia, who in her passions and administrative talents equaled the most powerful man; the reign of Maria Theresa, whose gallant Hungarians shouted "We will die for our king, Maria Theresa;" the reigns of the princesses of France, who ruled in defiance of the Salic law, these and many others Dr. Bushnell does not mention at all. He could not, and yet prove that women-rulers have been failures. If history proves anything, it proves that women of one type have talent for government, and have been among the most powerful rulers of the earth. But it suits Dr. Bushnell's purpose to declare that none of these sovereign women were great. Where they approximated to greatness, it was only because they "reflected men!" Elizabeth of England was not a great ruler, because she showed weaknesses as a woman. Judged by this standard, which man ruler among all was ever great? Do we find one, even among the most powerful, who did not at some time betray personal littleness? Then Frederic the Great was not a great king, because he was a literary pedant, and quarreled with Voltaire, and was shabby to his sister. Napoleon was not great, because he was devoured by envy, and was jealous of a woman's intellect all his life. Surely, he was *not* great when he so far forgot the gentleness of a gentleman as to push Madame De Staël behind him, that she might not enter a room before him.

Dr. Bushnell discusses his question from beginning to end entirely in reference to a theoretic man and woman. Most people carry an ideal man and woman in their head. And when the practical relations of the man and woman of every day are discussed with reference only to these impossible ideals, we need not marvel at any ridiculous conclusion. Dr. Bushnell's "woman" is a wondrous compound of violet and mignonnette, of angelic and of imbecile qualities. In one chapter she abides in "a sphere of silence;" in another she is a husband-hunter of the leap-year sort; in another she is "elected to gentleness and patience," or "to the dreadful lot of violence and tyrant-cruelty;" in every one she is an abject "subject." His "man" roars loosely through every page of the book. "Thunder" is a pet word with Dr. Bushnell. He would make us believe that at least every other man we meet is a Jupiter, emitting thunderbolts at every breath. He says: "It is the heavy tread, the *thundering guttural voice, the Jupiter-like air and expression (and man is not to blame for these)*," [no, poor fellow] that pass the law of female subordination. Then he gently asks his feminine compound of botanical and seraphic properties, "why she should wish to encroach upon this man's thunder-force?" Heaven forbid! What woman would not gladly perform a painful pilgrimage, if so she could but find her Jove, and then fall down and worship him! Alas! the actual Jupiters are very scarce. Somehow the average man has missed the godlike proportion both in mind and stature. Very often he is little more than a bundle of unreasoning prejudices, opinions, and passions; arrogating to himself utter supremacy simply through the fact of being a man, not from any mental or moral height which he has reached as an individual soul. Yet no less "this masculine half-being must be allowed to sink into the bigger self that he calls home, and be sheltered in the womanly peace." He finds it very pleasant, yet not more pleasant than the "womanly peace" finds it to shelter and to love him. Few are the women who would not choose to take this "half-being," disagreeable as he sometimes finds it possible to make himself, and abide in his protection as does he in her ministration. It is not possible. No amount of fine theorizing annuls the fact that tens of thousands of women must shape their own fortunes and take care of themselves. In England, in 1861, 840,000 married women supported themselves and their children by their own labor. This is a hard fact to set against Dr. Bushnell's remedy of universal marriages, to be accomplished through the workings of a gigantic matrimonial intelligence office, and a perpetual leap-year privilege accorded to woman to propose marriage to men. If anything could astonish one in Dr. Bushnell's book, it would be that so wise a man could be so foolish. Which would be the more unwomanly in woman, to represent herself as a human being and citizen, or to so far outrage the finest instincts of her womanhood as to offer herself, by indirect act or avowed word, to a man who had never sought her? What more degrades woman to-day than that she so often seeks marriage as a support? Why is the holy sacrament of love, the sanctity of the family state, so often prostituted and destroyed, but because marriage is entered upon as a necessity or a convenience? And what can so place marriage on its only true basis of mutual love, mutual fitness, mutual esteem, as for woman to make herself independent of it as a mere means of subsistence?

If woman was in fact the "subject" creature which Dr. Bushnell describes, she would not demand for herself and her children what she demands to-day. After so many centuries of travail, it would be a sad conclusion to come to, that the human family had not struggled upward to a higher and completer development. Such development could not come to one half of the human race alone. Amid all the blind groping of women toward something brighter and better, amid all the mistakes and extravagances which they commit, the fact that woman as woman demands for herself the complete right to herself, to the use of all her faculties as a human being, is the most hopeful promise of the time for the future of the whole human family. Man for so many ages has told her what to do, what not to do, what she was capable of doing and being, what she was not capable of doing or being, that to hear her declare for herself what she can do, what she has a right to do, what in God's good time she will do, is an invasion on precedent which he does not excuse or pardon. All his instincts and prejudices are armed against such innovation. For this reason every magazine and newspaper that we take up bristles with his deprecations, his warnings, his sneers, his injunctions, and his old, old story of what woman *is* and what she *is not*. Just here lies the lesson which the men of this age must learn. It is the core of the whole "Woman Question." The time has come for woman to decide for herself what she is and what she is not, to prove by opportunity what she can do and what she cannot do. Every human being carries the limitations of its action in its own constitution. It holds in its own consciousness the indice of its special, individual work. No outside soul can decide what that work is, — what its limitations are. No woman could completely represent a man. No man can represent a woman. He has tried to do it for centuries, and the result proves his utter incapacity. His very difference from her makes it impossible. The hour has come for woman to represent herself. Heretofore man has shut against her the gates of advancement and of culture open to himself. He has oppressed her with unequal laws, and *then* told her she was his inferior. Heretofore she has been measured and judged without half a chance as a human being. Hereafter she is to be measured and judged by her chance. Hereafter her development must be measured by the limits of her physical and mental constitution. How far those limits disqualify her for any employment or place can only be proved by free competition. It remains yet to be proved what those limits are. There may be a few mistaken women, who imagine that some height is to be gained by women seeking to be as men. Underlying this excrescence is the vast underlying need already voiced into a universal cry — the woman's need of free development, growth, opportunity, *as woman.* Harmony of organization, perfection of function, subtle fineness of brain-fibre, earnestness of soul, devotion of heart, spirituality *untrammeled*, must ever be the best feminine forces which she can bring to the world's service. No thoughtful, far-seeing woman, however she may admit the justice of equal suffrage, believes for one moment that she can find her *highest* enfranchisement in the casting of the ballot.

XXII.

"UNA AND HER PAUPERS."

"UNA and her paupers" is the designation given by Florence Nightingale to her whose name I once more lift up for the sake of other women, especially for that of my own countrywomen. Says Florence Nightingale of her: —

"One woman has died — a woman attractive, and rich, and young, and witty; yet a veiled and silent woman, distinguished by no other genius but the divine genius, working hard to train herself, in order to train others to walk in the footsteps of Him who went about doing good.

"She died, as she lived, at her post in one of the largest workhouse infirmaries in this kingdom, the first in which trained nursing has been introduced. She is the pioneer of workhouse nursing. I do not give her name; were she alive, she would beg me not. Of all human beings I have ever known, she was (I was about to say) the most free from the desire of the praise of men. But I cannot say the *most* free, for she was perfectly free. I will therefore call her Una, if you please; for, when her whole life and image rise before me, so far from thinking the story of Una and her lion a myth, I say here is Una in real flesh and blood — Una and her paupers, more untamable than lions." "She lived the life and died the death of the saints and martyrs, though the greatest sinner would not have been more surprised than she to have heard this said of herself. In less than three years she had reduced one of the most disorderly hospital populations in the world to something like Christian discipline, such as the police themselves wondered at. She had led to be of one mind and heart with her upward of fifty nurses and probationers. She had converted a vestry to the conviction of the economy as well as the humanity of nursing pauper sick by trained nurses. She had converted the poor-law board, a body not usually given to much enthusiasm about Unas and paupers. She had disarmed all opposition, all sectarian zealotism; so that Roman Catholic and Unitarian, High Church and Low Church, rose up and called her blessed. All, of all shades of religious creed, seemed to have merged their differences in her, seeing in her *the one true essential thing*, compared with which they acknowledged their differences to be as nothing.

"In less than three years — the time generally given to the ministry of that Saviour whom she so earnestly strove closely to follow — she did all this. She had the gracefulness, the wit, the unfailing cheerfulness — qualities so remarkable, but so much overlooked in our Saviour's life. She had the absence of all asceticism or mortification which characterized His work, and any real work in the present day, as in his day.

"All last winter she had under her charge above 50 nurses, above 150 pauper scourers, from 1,290 to 1,350 patients, being from two to three hundred more than the number of beds. All these she had to provide and arrange for, often receiving an influx of patients without a moment's warning. Among them were prostitutes, worn-out thieves, worn-out drunkards. No small portion of her work was to see that the dissolute and desperate did not corrupt the young and not hopelessly fallen. . . . . How did she do it all? She did it simply by the *manifestation of the life that was within her*, the trained, well-ordered life of doing her Father's business, so different from the governing, the ordering about, the driving principle. Everybody recognized it — the paupers, the vestry, the nurses, the poor-law board. The nurses would have died for her, because they always felt that she cared for them — for each one in herself — solely for their well-being. Because she had no care of praise in her, she had a greater power of carrying her followers with her than any woman or man I ever knew. . . . .

"We hear much of idle hands and unsatisfied hearts. All England is ringing with the cry for 'Woman's Work' and 'Woman's Mission.' Why are there so few to *do* the work? If any one would know what are the lowest depths of human vice and misery, would see the festering mass of decay of living human bodies and human souls, and then would try what one loving soul, filled with the spirit of her God, can do to let in the light of God into this hideous well, let her study the ways and follow in the steps of this one young, frail woman, who died to show us the way, blessed in her death as in her life."

"Dear Agnes" she was called by high and low, rich and poor. One who knew her always writes of her: —

"There are many who can look back upon her from the time when, in her own bright home, in the North of Ireland, she gave her days to tend the poor, where her visit was looked for as a ray of light beaming on body and soul. From those walks which would have annihilated most young ladies she would return, often amid drenching rains, as fresh as a rose to the social evening circle, ever devoted to the service and pleasure of all around her.

"We love to remember her in her home at Fahan, by the side of Lough Swilly, or among the glorious rocks of Port Rush, or as she guided us over the wide sea-floors of the Giant's Causeway; but we knew her better, and the memories of her are dearer, as in after days she threaded the close courts and alleys of the back streets of our great city, when she took voluntary share in the toils and cares and joys of our London Bible Mission."

Yet of this young *home* missionary her sister, who writes her memorials, says: "Of her it might indeed be said, whatever her hand found to do she did it with her might. She saw —

what many, alas! of the good and useful people of the present day fail to see — that God may be obeyed and glorified as truly in the small details of domestic life as in the greatest missionary work abroad."

Such a life as this bears me back to the deep, sweet fountains of womanly character which fed my childhood — to such women as Susannah Wesley, Mary Fletcher, Madame Guion, Catherine Adorna, Ann and Sarah Judson, and Margaret Prior, of New York. In this loud, egotistical day it comes with a touch of healing. It is a benediction in the air, hushing discord into peace. Listening to its lesson, in the presence of God's poor and sick, one must marvel that so many women of means, of leisure, who fill the world with their outcry for "opportunity" and work, who rebel against the meagreness and littleness of their pursuits, do not see how broad are the fields, how wonderful the harvest of bodies and of souls, waiting, wasting for woman's touch of mercy. I would not be understood as urging romantic, enthusiastic, untaught women into *any* mode of life for which they are constitutionally unfitted. But I wish it were in my power (though I doubt if it is) to say one word to make more desirable to the mass of dissatisfied, unoccupied, affluent women the education which would fit them for, in varied phases, a life of benevolent labor. There is no more painful sign of the times than the restlessness, the dissatisfaction, the lamenting, and yet the idleness of this class. Women who must work for their living are saved a thousand horrors which beset Fortune's (nominally) more favored children. "I envy you because you are so *busy*," said one. "Oh! if I only had something of *importance to do*, to make me forget little, miserable annoyances." Does that lovely, unhappy woman see an "importance" worth the seeking in the life of Sister Agnes? It was not an easy life. Oh! no. Is that why so few comparatively seek it? Its rewards never take the sound of public applause. Is that why Florence Nightingale must cry: "Oh! daughters of God, are there so few to answer?" A growing passion for publicity is fast becoming the bane of American women. They scarcely realize it; yet it is becoming a prevailing fact that no vocation seems to them to be worth their seeking unless they think that in some way it will recompense them with applause or "fame." What a pitiful mistake! I say this in no way underrating the gift of utterance, the power to embody in color or form any work of imperishable genius. I am glad for every woman who does well, be it on stage, or forum. God never endows a creature with any gift without his purpose — beyond man's finding out. Yet no less the mass of women, aye, and of men, must perform their life-work in silence. They must do their work, whatever that work may be, and find reward simply in its doing. God is just. Woman has come to her day. The feminine soul will take its half of the universe. Yet no less the women who thrill our hearts, before whose very memory we bow in reverence, have done their highest work unconsciously. "They builded better than they knew."

Do you ask which of all is the happiest life? Then I say, from my heart, a consecrated one. Be it "in the world" (so called) or out of it, in highway or by-way, as God wills, still a life consecrated to a service better, higher, sweeter than that of self-enjoyment or self-success. We all want to be happy. We all seek personal joy as an instinct. Surely, God meant it to be thus when HE made us. Yet no less HE has set the deepest sources of joy outside of self-indulgence — in love, obedience, devotion, and duty. It may be a hard word, the last; it has a chilly sound. Yet no less it claims and possesses us more and more as our days go on. Impulse, desire, idolatry, aggressive selfhood — one by one we lay them down. We drop our weights as we go upward. Lo! the cross that we called Duty changes to our crown.

XXIII.

LET US LIVE.

I OPEN my window upon the world just wakened, and wonder if in any supreme moment I was ever thankful enough for the great boon of existence. It is so wonderful to be alive! It is so blessed to live. "Yes," said a friend to me once, "if we did not have to die; but this world which you delight in so much — the trail of death is over it all." He had buried in the earth the delight of his eyes and the love of his life. Silence was my duty, standing within the shadow of that loss. Yet I do not delight in life because I am unacquainted with grief. I am pervaded with the consciousness of the impending mystery of death — the awful change to the one taken, the desolation to those left. I lift my weights and move on, often with an unsteady step. I see my friends falter and fall down beneath their crosses. Struggle, strife, treachery, disappointment, loss, anguish, hopelessness — the night-shade of human life — I do not forget it; I cannot. The very shadow that it casts — the long, long shadow, often stretching across nearly all the weary space from the cradle to the grave — makes me sure that to few, very few is human life the boon that it might be. I forgot nothing, not even inherited taint, moral, intellectual, spiritual; the *fate* in temperament, which is the saddest curse entailed upon perverted humanity. But, after weighing all in the balance, still I am sure that just to live, under ordinary conditions, is a privilege of which we but rarely make the most; a possibility to whose highest limit we can but seldom rise. We find only at intervals the inevitable doom a drawback to our joy. Usually it is the care, the worry, the torment, which should not have occurred at all. We have gone so far from Nature. Our lives are so artificial, so false, or so petty. Our great sorrows, like our great opportunities, stand far apart, lonely landmarks in our lives. And it is humiliating to sum up the meagre frets which make the discontent and unhappiness of average daily life. Your new dress fits miserably; therefore, for the time being, you must be wholly miserable. John thumbs the walls and bangs the doors, and you grow overwrought and wretched.

Your husband comes home at night silent,

cold, or cross. All day you have been thinking what a dear fellow he is. He did a splendid deed yesterday, over which you fondly muse. Nobody on earth is quite so fine, or noble, or wholly to be adored as he. He opens the door. Lo! your god is a moody man. Something has gone wrong — his digestion, very likely. He ate a piece of pie in a restaurant at noon vile enough to tear up mucous membrane and temper together. He is blind to all the little love surprises that you have lying in wait for him. He knocks down your bouquet, smashes your vase, bungles and bangs generally. In the keen reaction of disappointment, you answer him shortly or sharply. He in his turn says something which indicates that he does not think you altogether an angel. Either of you would die for the other. No less, each wonders for the moment how the other can be so disagreeable. What a perfect evening you had pictured to be spent together. You spend it apart. It ends in tears and sullenness. You dump your head on your pillow and wonder why you were born.

You leave your work at night, thinking all the way home what a dear wife awaits you there. They are all present with you, a hundred graces and goodnesses of hers, of whom nobody else dreams. You think of them, and how much she loves you, till you wonder in penitence how you could ever for a moment have been neglectful or unkind. "Never, never will I be again," says the spontaneous heart as you open your door on your angel at an unlucky moment. She has just spanked Tom, and is still shaking Susan. Such a day! Servants, children, markets, and shops all awry. She *is* a darling. Some other time she will make you sure of it, and beguile you with most delicious chatter and laughter; but not now. She is wearied, worried, and irritable — overworked, in fine. You could soothe her in a minute, if you would; but you won't. You believe in the ancient tradition that "a wife should *always* meet her husband with a smile." She should always hide her troubles out of *his* sight. You remind her of this. You tell her that she is "unreasonable." She retorts bitterly that she "wishes you could be a woman for an hour." With a superior air, you inform her that you would not be a woman for a moment, upon any consideration. You spend the evening away from home. Nevertheless, you find your pantaloons mended in the morning, and look upon them with a pricking of conscience, that would deepen could you see the sad tears that dropped into the stitches. You over-eat, or under-eat, or eat at the wrong time. Your headaches, your nerves are like needles, your words are disagreeable, even while the soul within you is yearning for perfection. Perhaps, like poor Eugénie de Guerin, you have a soul that "afflicts itself about the least thing. A word, a memory, a tone of voice, a sad expression, a nameless nothing, will often disturb the serenity of your spirit — small sky that the lightest cloud can tarnish."

The processions of the seasons pass on. The constellations march through space. Days die in serenity and are born in splendor. The universe lavishes its largess for your delight; yet, of the infinite that it gives, how little you take in, how much less you assimilate. In what poverty you abide. What scanty measure you give out.

In what perception, or faculty, or emotion do you rise to the supreme fullness of life? You are haunted with the consciousness of what you miss, of what you have never reached. What dulls and deadens and irritates you this moment? Pickles and preserves, festering together in your stomach, very likely. Dyspepsia may be the penalty of long-violated laws. Or some discord of noises, or of souls, which you cannot prevent. Something, a petty or mean little something, doubtless; yet it is mighty enough to undermine resolves, to defraud you of the highest and finest essence of life; more, to rob you of the possession of your highest and sweetest self. Nor is the victim scarcely ever wholly to blame. The most exquisite flavor of daily existence eludes us chiefly through the lack of a prevailing and pervading courtesy in our constant intercourse with each other; through a careless lack of tender consideration for the temperamental differences and infirmities which exist in all. —— is "foolish and has notions;" that is reason sufficient why —— should be crossed, and by so much in no wise considered. We dismiss the fact without study, without one atom of tender feeling, and treat the victim accordingly. Think how many loudly-professing "friends" you have who never fail to repeat a cutting, sarcastic, or even rude remark; who just as rarely speak to you one kind or encouraging word. It is a sad comment on human nature that the one who repeats an uncharitable speech is invariably considered sincere, while the person who ventures to repeat or express a very kindly one is always open to the suspicion of flattery.

This lack of courtesy, of sympathetic kindness in little things, is surely the bane of average daily life. We see it, feel it, suffer from it everywhere. It is as culpably palpable in the highest council of the nation as it is in the humblest household.

Yes, Swedenborg's doctrine is true. We in our lower state are infested with demons — the demons of selfishness, which hold us down from the fullness and perfectness of human existence. Yet the soul will not be defrauded altogether of its birthright. Sometimes it soars and takes possession of its high estate. Then you know what it is to be glad to live. In some clear dawn, in some still night, in some moment of rest, when you possess your soul in peace, you realize it all — the bliss of being, the joy of breathing, the ministry of light, of color, of odor, of sound, the ecstasy of inspiration, the presence of God. What is it not, the heart in you that loves and lifts its idol up into the light of supernal faith, where it abides transfigured, sanctified, and safe from sin? What is it not, this yearning for knowledge, this hunger for the perfect, this reaching out toward the illimitable, this capacity to love, to suffer, to renounce, to believe, to know, to aspire, and to strive upward toward the aspiration? All this may be shut in one weary frame, even under a stove-pipe hat or a fashionable bonnet. Every breeze that stirs, every bird that sings, every flower that blooms, every moment, with its utmost perfect possibility, — is my minister, a portion of the universal joy of life. Get thee behind me, world — the world of mean cares, of self-love, of petty strifes, of poor ambitions! Give me that which is holy and eternal — the kind word, the unselfish deed, the care for others in little things, the charity that can suffer and yet be kind, the affection which, sweetening life and surviving death, is our only foretaste of Heaven.